"MISSION COVID-19"
THE QUANTUM EFFECT

"MISSION COVID-19"

THE QUANTUM EFFECT

NICKLOIS LEONARD

gatekeeper press™
Columbus, Ohio

The Quantum Effect "Mission COVID-19"

Published by Gatekeeper Press
2167 Stringtown Rd, Suite 109
Columbus, OH 43123-2989
www.GatekeeperPress.com

Library of Congress Control Number: 2020947916

ISBN (hardcover): 9781662907500
ISBN (paperback): 9781662904905
eISBN: 9781662904912

I would like to dedicate this book to my heavenly Father who above all gave me the strength, inspiration and time for me to write this book.

I would also like to dedicate this book to my beautiful wife Amy who through her love and support continued to encourage me to pursue my long-term goal of becoming an author. I love you Honey Bear!

Contents

CHAPTER 1

QSTCC: Quantum Space-Time Continuum Command

Present Day

COMMANDING OFFICER CLINT Maxwell and Command Master Chief Paul Mitchell entered the room and logged onto the computer, then sat in two of the leather chairs around the table. The briefing room was brightly lit, with no windows. Pictures hanging on three of the four walls featured some of the greatest discoveries originating out of Area 51. An image of an SR-71 Blackbird was mounted on the back wall, along with pictures of a U-2 spy plane and an F-117 Nighthawk. The conference table was large, handcrafted, and oval-shaped in oak with twelve matching chairs. In the center was a speakerphone connected to a secure line. Directly above the speaker was a video projector mounted to the ceiling, and on the opposite side of the room, sitting on an unassuming desk, was the computer that provided the secure connection to the National Security Team files related to the mission objectives.

"Good morning, Master Chief!" said Clint. "Are you and the team settling into our new location?"

"Good morning and yes sir, the team and I are getting acquainted with our new surroundings," replied Paul. "Thanks for asking."

"Do you realize it'll be fifteen years next month that we both went through BUD/S together?"

Paul leaned back in his chair and stretched his legs, ran his fingers through his short salt-and-pepper hair, and said, "Well sir, I really hadn't thought much about it, to be honest. It seems like such a long time ago. A lot of water under the bridge since then."

"I agree. But oh, what a ride it's been, my friend." Clint paused and then continued, "Master Chief, I have orders from General Lawless to start reviewing the potential mission files from the National Security Team, and provide him with a list of the first three missions we want to embark on to get our feet wet."

Paul tilted his head to the side, confused. "I'm not sure that's how this is supposed to work. I mean, shouldn't General Lawless decide what missions we need to act on?"

"The QSTCC is so new, the National Security Team hasn't figured out when and how to execute the missions listed in the database. General Lawless wants us to provide a list of potential missions instead. By tomorrow."

"Seems a little unorthodox if you ask me. But if that's what the general wants, who are we to argue?"

"Well, let's see what they've collected so far, shall we?" Clint booted up the computer files and displayed them on the projector screen. "Looks like there are at least twenty-five potential mission files listed here." He quietly laughed, shaking his head. "Check out some of these titles. 'California Secedes from the Union.' 'The Northwest Exodus.' 'COVID-19 Cover-Up.' '9-11 Cover-Up.' 'United States Second Civil War.' Damn!"

Paul leaned back in his chair and took a long sip of his coffee. "Who in their right mind would come up with mission names like these?"

"Well, Master Chief, let's not be too hard on the National Security Team. After all, they're the ones who gave us this new assignment." Clint stood up and walked to the coffee machine. "Refill?"

"No, I think I've had enough for now. Let's get this review over with so I can get back to setting up our new base of operations."

"Okay. Let's look at this one titled 'COVID-19 Cover-Up.'" Clint opened the file to the mission overview section. "It looks like the scope of this mission is to determine the lengths pharmaceutical executives and government officials have gone to, in collusion, to accomplish four major objectives. First, create a worldwide emergency to ensure the American people will panic, allowing the government to infringe on their constitutional rights by means of public safety. Second, destroy the economy by enforcing quarantine protocol, forcing most companies to lay off employees, raising unemployment numbers prior to the 2020 election. Third, create a major source of revenue for hospitals treating everyone for COVID-19 regardless of cause, along with money for the research and development of a fake vaccine to benefit the pharmaceutical companies. And finally, our fourth objective is to determine whether multiple countries around the world colluded to destabilize the US administration and return to the old status quo."

Paul blurted out a little laugh. "This frankly sounds like some of the conspiracy theories I read as the pandemic was just getting started. I also heard that a large crackdown on the human trafficking ring among celebrities and politicians was a major reason the government wanted us to all remain indoors, so we couldn't see what was really going on. And mobile hospital ships were deployed to treat the trafficking victims, not COVID patients."

Clint shook his head. "That's a lot to swallow, don't you think, Master Chief? I mean, sure, I read all those conspiracy theories too, but this is America. We don't treat our citizens that way. We're a civilized society that follows the rule of law. That's what makes it possible to function."

Both men looked at each other, then suddenly broke up in laughter. Paul regained his composure first. "Let me get this straight. Our government wants us to use the Quantum Space-Time Continuum Command to run down conspiracy theories?"

"It appears so, Master Chief. So, we need to go through these files and provide the general with the three best missions to help our team get their feet wet."

The two began reviewing each case file, rating it for potential inclusion on the short list, when they came across one labeled "SEAL Team 2 Disaster."

"Skipper, that file label doesn't make any sense," said Paul. "We're SEAL Team 2. Or at least we were."

"You can see the file is different from the rest. It's labeled 'For National Security Team Eyes ONLY.' I'm not sure this one is supposed to be here."

"If they didn't want us to see this file, why would it be here?"

Clint stared at the projector screen for a good twenty seconds, gathering his thoughts before he replied, "Hell, we're doing things here I never could have even dreamed of until a couple of weeks ago. Let's see what lies behind door number one, shall we?"

Clint clicked on the file to open it. What appeared next was a quick summary of what had occurred while SEAL Team 2 was on its mission in Wuhan.

"This case file states that three personnel from our team were killed while trying to extract Dr. Shun." Clint started reading the report out loud in a calm but firm voice. "The team arrived at Dr. Shun's apartment just after the Chinese military, which resulted in a firefight to secure the subject. During the assault, Lieutenant Wise, Senior Chief Barnes, PO1 Beachier, and Dr. Shun were all killed."

Clint and Paul looked at each other in complete disbelief. "I can't believe what I'm reading, Skipper. This doesn't make any sense."

Paul paused, visibly shaken, then stood. "I'm heading back to my office, to officially forget what you just read to me. I refuse to believe that we would've made such a basic error as to cause the death of three of our own team members." He walked out the door, leaving Clint with the open file.

Clint didn't try to stop him. He knew that he needed to give Paul some time to process the information. After all, this was just theory, right? He continued to review the file, to see if there was anything that could have been done differently. After an hour, he returned to his office to ponder what he had just read.

* * *

Paul returned to his office to work through some of the logistical challenges the team would face over the next few weeks, but his mind kept going back to the briefing room earlier that morning. Sitting at his desk, he couldn't stop thinking about the SEAL Team 2 Disaster case file that Commander Maxwell had discovered in the database.

He went to the bathroom sink, splashed water on his face, then looked up into the mirror and thought to himself, *We can't ignore the intel in the database, but what if it's wrong? What if it never really happened in the first place? Or, what if it already did?* He grabbed a towel, dried himself off, then headed over to Clint's office.

Clint had been sitting in his office for the past couple of hours, also thinking about the case file. He stood up and started to pace back and forth, talking out loud to himself. "What if this really did happen?" He paused. "We know for a fact that it didn't, because we're all here today. There's no way that this disaster could've taken place." Another long pause. "Right?"

He suddenly stopped, a major revelation coming to him. "Wait, of course! This is exactly what General Lawless was talking about!"

Just then there was a knock on the door, and Paul entered. "We need to talk."

"Come on in, Master Chief. Yes, you're right, we do."

"I was thinking that maybe the reason this mission was included in the files is because General Lawless knew we wouldn't allow our team to be harmed without a fight."

"I came to the same conclusion. If you remember, the team said you and I were in Dr. Shun's apartment just as they breached the door."

"Yes, but how does that explain the mission file?"

Clint paused for a few seconds and sat down in his chair. "I think it's clear that our first mission is saving the lives of our team—you and me, specifically."

"Why us?"

"Because we weren't there. We were onboard the submarine. It makes perfect sense."

"Clint, are you sure about all of this? I mean, what if you're wrong?"

Clint stood silently looking at Paul for a moment,, then shook his head. "I'm not sure, but we can't sit idly by and let this happen. We need to do something."

"What about authorization? This clearly isn't one of the official mission choices."

"I'm the commanding officer of the QSTCC, and I can authorize whatever mission I deem suitable." Clint paused for a moment, then added, "Master Chief, just before General Lawless left a few days ago, he gave me a folder with a single sheet of paper inside it. I thought it was some kind of joke or something, but the general was adamant about me taking it to heart."

Paul looked puzzled. "What did the paper say?"

Clint opened his safe, pulled out the folder, and showed Paul the paper. In simple ballpoint handwriting, it said, "You will know it when you see it."

Both Clint and Paul stood there processing the message for a moment. Finally, Clint put the file away, saying, "Master Chief, we are moving forward with this operation."

"Agreed. But we need a plan."

"Well, you're the expert on mission planning, Paul. What are your thoughts?"

"Okay, let me think for a second." Paul walked over to Clint's whiteboard and started to draw on it. "Based on the case file, we know that the Chinese military arrived at Dr. Shun's apartment shortly before our team arrived. My suggestion is we use the quantum transporter to teleport us into Dr. Shun's apartment just before our team breaches the door for extraction."

Clint interrupted him. "We'll need to know the exact time the team performed the breach. I believe we can use the QVSR to figure that out."

Paul wrote that on the board and continued. "Before we step through the event horizon of the quantum transporter, we throw a couple of flash grenades to immobilize anyone who's currently in the room. Next, we step through the event horizon into Dr. Shun's apartment. I'll do a security sweep to ensure everyone is unconscious while you check to verify that Dr. Shun is still alive."

Clint clasped his hands together excitedly. "Affirmative, Master Chief. I like your plan. But we need to be fast. If we time this correctly, we'll have less than a minute to step through the event horizon, secure the area, check on Dr. Shun, and ensure the team returns safely for the mission to be a success. Once our team breaches the door, I'll follow you back through the event horizon. The door breach will validate that our team is safe."

A large smile spread across Paul's face. "I like this plan, Clint. Let's get this party started!"

From that moment forward, the team trained 24/7 using technology to simulate every possible scenario and outcome. After two weeks of nonstop planning, revising, updating, testing, and re-testing, they were ready.

Both Paul and Clint knew what had to be done. The first trip through the quantum transporter would be them!

*   *   *

Lieutenant Thomas Wise, the officer in charge of QSTCC ground operations, opened the door to the lab on sublevel ten, underneath the main admin building at Area 51. "Dr. Maxwell!" he shouted. "Are you in here?"

Dr. Grace Maxwell was conducting system checks over by the quantum transporter. "I'm over here, Lieutenant. And please, call me Grace. I'm not old enough yet for Dr. Maxwell."

"Grace it is, then." Tom strolled over and stood by her, looking the transporter up and down. "This machine is like nothing I've ever seen before. I mean, I used to watch a lot of science fiction when I was younger, but this truly takes the cake. Did you design it?"

Grace put down her clipboard and turned to him. "Well, technically I did, but I had a lot of help from Dr. Rubin. So, what brings you down to the lab?"

"I was curious to how the system actually works."

Grace thought to herself, *This could be fun.* "Would you like me to walk you through the process, Lieutenant?"

"Absolutely! I want to know what makes this baby tick!"

Grace chuckled, then pointed at the control panel. "This is the main operations panel that controls all functionality of the quantum transporter." She walked over to the side and continued her show-and-tell. "This is one of the four ion cannons that actually creates the wormhole-like event horizon that the team steps through." She then walked over to one of the nearby tables and grabbed what looked like a clunky wristwatch. "This is the device that links the traveler back to our current timeline. We call it the beacon. Once each of you is wearing one, we dial up the control panel to the exact time and location where the team will go, and then we activate the quantum transporter. The wormhole links you to that point in time where we want you to go, you step through the event horizon, and *poof!* you're there! Once you're on the other side, the beacon allows us to monitor your location, establish communication, and bring you back through the event horizon into our timeline. Any questions?"

Tom stood there with his mouth open. "I can't believe this actually works."

"I assure you, Lieutenant, it works quite well."

"Will we be able to call up the wormhole ourselves with these beacon thingies?" asked Tom, fondling the device.

Grace sighed. "Unfortunately, no, at least not yet. In order for you to come back to our current time, we must have regular check-in times with you, to ensure we can open the event horizon and allow you to step through when you're ready to return. I've been working on a device that should be able to link back to the quantum transporter and allow you to open the event horizon yourself, but it's not ready yet."

The telephone started ringing and Grace picked it up. "Lab, Maxwell."

"Dr. Maxwell, this is Master Chief Mitchell. Head down to the transporter room and meet Commander Maxwell and me there, ASAP."

"What seems to be the problem?"

"No time to waste, Dr. Maxwell. Just please meet us there as soon as you can make it."

Grace hung up the phone and said to Tom, "That was a strange call. Master Chief Mitchell just told me to report to the transporter room as quickly as possible. Do you know what's going on?"

Tom got a puzzled look on his face. "Grace, I never have any idea what's going on around here. I guess I'll find out the same time as you."

* * *

Five minutes later, the four were assembled in the transporter room. "What's this all about, Clint?" asked Grace.

Clint handed her the mission brief and said, "We're going to save our team, Grace. I need you to dial up these coordinates on the QVSR, give us the exact time we need to transport to, and then operate the quantum transporter for us to enter the event horizon." He noticed Tom standing by the operations panel. "Lieutenant, head back up to HQ and ensure you have all the equipment our team needs for our up-and-coming missions."

"Commander, is there something wrong?" Tom asked. "Anything I can help with here?"

"No, Lieutenant, nothing that the Master Chief and I can't handle. I'll see you this afternoon at our usual mission briefing."

"Yes, sir."

Grace looked down at the document. "How did you get your hands on this, Clint? I'm sorry, but I can't allow you to conduct this operation."

"Grace, you don't have a choice. I'm the commanding officer here. Get the information from the QVSR that

I've requested, then warm up the quantum transporter and prepare for deployment."

Grace continued standing there in disbelief. "Clint, we haven't sent a real person through the quantum transporter yet! It's too dangerous!"

Clint raised his voice. "Grace! I said dial up the quantum transporter to the location I provided you!"

She looked over the brief again. "You don't even know if this actually happened. Are you and Master Chief honestly prepared to take the risk?"

"Of course it happened. It's right there in black and white. If we don't go back and execute this mission, the case file will come true and neither I nor the Master Chief will be able to live with the knowledge that we could have prevented it."

Grace stared at the two of them one more time, then went over to the QVSR and began to carry out Clint's request. "I have the data you requested from the QVSR. I'm putting it into the quantum transporter now."

Clint looked at Paul for confirmation that he was ready, then shouted, "Initiate transporter protocol, Grace! Do it now!"

Grace reluctantly energized the quantum transporter, creating a glowing ring that hovered in the air in front of them. Paul shouted, "Are you ready, Skipper?"

"Arm the flash grenades and let's do this!"

Clint and Paul each threw live flash grenades through the event horizon, waited a couple of seconds, then stepped through. Once they were on the other side, they confirmed that the grenades had done their job, immobilizing everyone in Dr. Shun's apartment.

"Master Chief, verify everyone is unconscious. I'll look for the good doctor."

"You're the boss, Skipper."

Paul scurried about, confirming that all the Chinese soldiers in the room were unconscious. Clint surveyed the room and found the doctor, checking for a pulse to make sure he was still alive.

They heard the SEAL team approaching the door from the other side. "Master Chief!" yelled Clint. "Prepare to exit!"

"Let's go, Skipper! Move your ass!"

The two headed towards the glowing ring just as the door opened. Clint ran through the transporter with Paul right behind him; then suddenly the ring was gone, leaving only Dr. Shun and a pile of unconscious Chinese soldiers when the SEAL team burst through the door.

CHAPTER 2

Where It All Began

I N THE SUMMER of 2019, the President added the Space Force as the fifth branch of the United States military. From then through 2020, both private industry and the government discovered and developed several new and exciting technologies. One such invention never shared with the public was in the area of quantum physics, discovered by Dr. Hans Rubin, a brilliant physicist born and raised in Cleveland, Texas, just northeast of Houston. Dr. Rubin's current work assignment was at the infamous secret base in Nevada known as Area 51. His career in the Department of Defense was phenomenal until his wife passed of cervical cancer. Since Gina's death, Dr. Rubin had not been the same. He started taking more risks during experiments that he would have never even considered before his wife died.

On a beautiful spring day in May 2020, Dr. Rubin was working in his secret lab on a project which would prove the space-time continuum theory, permitting quantum-type travel. Hans was working with his assistant, the beautiful Dr. Grace Maxwell. Grace was tall, slender and physically fit, with long black hair that flowed halfway down her back. She had her mother's deep blue eyes and a smile that lit up the world. A quantum physics PhD student from MIT, Grace was conducting her residency with Dr. Rubin, who happened to be the best friend of her father, Tony Maxwell.

"Grace, take my notes and assemble the photon emitter per my instructions," Dr. Rubin said as he handed her a notebook on that fateful day.

Grace started to review the document. "Yes, Doctor Rubin, I should be able to set up the equipment and be ready to conduct the test later this afternoon."

As the two prepared for the day's work, Hans went over the whole thing again. "To achieve a superposition of light particles being split, a group of three-way mirrors must be placed in position to see light at two distinct points of time. We need to ensure these mirrors are exactly aligned per my instructions."

Grace smiled. "And of course once we finish the mirror placement, we need to finish setting up the Hadron Collider. Then we'll be ready to start pretest checks."

Several hours and many prechecks later, they were finally ready. "Power up the Hadron Collider and establish the Higgs field," said Hans.

Grace reached over and flipped a switch. The Hadron Collider came alive and started to initialize the Higgs field when Grace noticed something wasn't right. "Doctor Rubin, the Higgs field appears to be destabilizing. I'm going to try to adjust to correct the issue."

"Be careful, Grace! We don't know what could happen if the Higgs field fails to hold. Be prepared to hit the emergency shutdown switch!"

While Grace was working to try to delocalize the Higgs field on the Hadron Collider, something unexpected happened. "Look!" she exclaimed. "Instead of seeing light at two distinct points of time, we're seeing a tear in the time-space continuum!"

Dr. Rubin was in complete amazement as well. "I believe you're correct, Grace. What exactly did you do?"

"I'm not sure, Doc, but I'll try to make some more adjustments."

"Grace, I'm not sure what's going on here. I need you to be very careful. We're dealing with something that has never been done at this magnitude before."

As Grace started making adjustments to the Hadron Collider, she noticed a new problem. "Doc! The power spikes are starting to go off the scales! I'm not sure how much longer I can control the Higgs field!"

The Higgs field continued to fluctuate outside the test parameters when a window suddenly appeared within the field. "Are you seeing this, Grace?" Hans excitedly said. "It looks like some sort of window. But to where?"

"Doc, I can't control the Higgs field anymore. I'm shutting it down."

But the Hadron Collider wasn't responding to the shutdown control sequence. Not exactly sure what was happening, Grace reached over and activated the emergency shutoff device for the Hadron Collider and stopped the test.

"Are you okay, Grace?" shouted Hans as he ran over to check on her.

"Yes, Doc, I'm fine."

"Quick thinking. You have your father's quick reaction skills."

Grace uttered confusedly, "What exactly did we do, Doc? I've never seen anything like that before. I mean, I could've sworn we opened up some sort of window."

"I'm completely taken aback as well. We need to turn the Hadron Collider back on to try to recreate what we just observed."

Regaining her composure, Grace replied, "Doc, normally I would agree with you, but honestly, I couldn't control the Higgs field. Our equipment either malfunctioned or something else occurred here. I insist we debrief and figure out if we damaged our equipment."

Hans knew she was right but still felt frustrated. "You're right, of course."

*   *   *

After several hours of verifying the lab equipment, Grace said, "Hey, Doc, I just finished my inspection of the equipment, and everything appears to be functioning normally."

"Are you sure our equipment didn't malfunction?"

Grace tilted her head. "Am I not the equipment expert here?"

Hans smiled. "Yes, you are, Grace. How could I ever doubt you?"

"Good. Now that we have that straight, I want to download the data from the Hadron Collider to a flash drive, and take it back to my office to run some analysis on it. I think I may be able to find out why I couldn't control the Higgs field, and just maybe we can determine what was inside it."

"Sounds like a great idea. Let me know if you find anything. I'll review my notes to see if I can find anything on my end."

Grace walked over to the Hadron Collider and downloaded the data to a flash drive for further analysis.

"Hey, Grace, make sure you run the data on that new Summit Supercomputer. We have to find out what caused the effects we observed today."

"Sounds good, Doc. Why don't you head back to your office and relax? Let me do some digging on the Summit Supercomputer. I'll let you know if I find anything."

Hans went back to his office at the other end of the lab. A cramped room full of reference books and a large oak desk in the center, this was where he spent most of his time since his wife passed.

He was still in shock after what he and Grace had just witnessed. Lots of things were running through his mind. When they met up later, after their individual examinations of the data, he began their conversation with a question he never imagined he'd actually ask out loud.

"Grace, do you think we could've opened a window into a different dimension in time-space? What was it we saw? Was it real? Was it a figment of our imagination? Was it an optical illusion? Was it our past or future? Would we be able to replicate it, or was this just a freak accident in the lab?"

Grace leaned back in her chair. "To be honest with you, Doc, I'm not sure what we saw. I mean, one minute I saw the Higgs field develop, then the next minute the system started having power surges. When I looked up at the Higgs field, I observed the same window you described. I've never seen anything like it either, so your concerns are certainly valid."

"Do you think it's possible that we opened a thread that entered into a different dimension of time or space? Quantum physics says it is possible, but no one has ever proven the theory."

"Tell you what, Doc, why don't you let me work with the Summit Supercomputer, crunch all the data, and let me get the answers we need? I'll have the computer run simulations to validate some of our theses. Will that make you happy?"

Dr. Rubin chuckled, smiled, and said, "Yes, Grace, that would make me happy."

But after Grace left his office, Hans admitted to himself what he hadn't been able to admit to her—they had proven beyond a shadow of doubt that humanity is now capable of opening a thread that enters a different dimension of time or space. All that was left now was for Grace to analyze the data and confirm it.

CHAPTER 3

The Team Departs for Wuhan

2020

COMMANDER CLINT MAXWELL was the current commander of Navy SEAL Team 2, stationed out of Naval Amphibious Base Little Creek in Virginia Beach, Virginia. A tall, slender man, he stood at six-three and weighed 235 pounds. He had short black hair, a black beard and mustache, and dark blue eyes. He was a ladies' man, for sure; he had never married. He didn't want someone worrying about him while he was out conducting missions.

On his way to the base in his brand-new GMC Sierra 2500HD Denali 4x4 diesel-fueled truck, Clint's phone rang. "Maxwell," he answered on the Bluetooth speaker.

"Good morning, Skipper!" It was Command Master Chief Paul Mitchell, calling to update him on the mission they were about to embark on. The team was getting ready to conduct an operation in China, in which they would extract a Chinese scientist who could supposedly confirm the source of the COVID-19 pandemic that had started a few months prior. "I hope you're coming to work ready to rock and roll today. The team's standing by the hangar, ready to head out. Just waiting on your slow ass. Uh, sir."

Clint smiled. "Nice to hear you have everything ready early as usual, Master Chief. ETA ten minutes."

The aircraft hangar was located on the north end of the airfield, providing security and cover for the team's operations. Inside the hangar was a large C-130 Hercules transport plane specially designed to shuttle the SEAL team anywhere in the world at a moment's notice. The plane was fueled, loaded, and ready to fly.

Clint arrived at the hangar and went into the front office, to discuss the makeup of the team with Paul before he addressed the others. "Good morning, Skipper!" Paul said. "Nice to see you found your way out to the hangar without your GPS."

Clint shook Paul's hand. "Nice to see you too, Master Chief. I'm curious to see who you've chosen for our operation."

Paul pulled out his notes and started going over the crew. "The officer in charge is Lieutenant Tom Wise. Born and raised in Charlotte, North Carolina. Graduated with honors from the Naval Academy with an electrical engineering degree, then top of his class at

BUD/S. A natural ability to lead and well respected by his teammates. He was the OIC (Officer in Charge) for several critical missions in Afghanistan and Iraq over the last couple of years. Known for courage under fire. If you remember, sir, Lieutenant Wise led a team into a hot LZ and rescued a helicopter crew after they were shot down by insurgents."

"Good choice for OIC, Master Chief. Who else made your best-of-the-best list?"

"Next is Senior Chief Bill Barnes as platoon chief for this mission. Born and raised on a dairy farm in southeast Ohio. Enlisted in the Navy right out of high school, number-one rated sailor in every class he attended, including BUD/S. Barnes is a highly qualified operator with numerous excursions into enemy territory. He was also the platoon chief that went into the hot LZ with Lieutenant Wise to rescue that helicopter crew. Another highly respected sailor within the teams, with fifteen years operational experience. Personally speaking, Barnes is one of the finest men I know, sir."

"I couldn't agree more, Master Chief. Bill was my communications specialist back when I was an OIC."

Paul continued, "Next on our list is Chief Brent Norton, our communications specialist. Norton was raised in a small town just outside Buffalo, New York. After high school, he enlisted in the Army for four years, then left and enlisted in the Navy. Said he needed a change, and the folks on the teams seemed like his kind of people. Top of his class in radio school and in BUD/S. He's proven himself capable under fire on many occasions. He was the operator who established communications during that FUBAR mission last year, if you remember, when the entire team was pinned down from heavy enemy fire."

"Yes," Clint said, frowning. "I certainly do remember that one."

"Norton placed his life on the line, single-handedly securing an antenna in the open bush to call in air support. With a bullet in his arm, he got the job done. He's fluent in three languages and highly respected by his fellow operators."

"Another fantastic pick, Paul. Please continue."

"Chief Ryan Nolan will be our advanced special operations coordinator. Nolan was born and raised in Huntsville, Texas. Graduated Texas A&M with honors as a petroleum engineer before enlisting in the Navy. Ranked number one in all of his Navy course programs, including BUD/S. Chief Nolan is an experienced operator who has planned and supported several highly complex rescue and extraction missions in the past three years. He's the best of the best when it comes to tactics. He's also highly respected among the teams. We're lucky to have him."

"I couldn't agree more. Who's next?"

"Petty Officer 1st Class Brian Beachier is our explosive ordnance disposal operator. Beachier was born and raised near a logging community on the outskirts of Colorado Springs, Colorado, where his family were loggers. He was raised around explosives and learned from his father. After high school, he decided to leave the logging business, wanted to be a part of something bigger, so he enlisted in the Navy. He was a top-notch student in all of his Navy classes, breaking records in disarming bombs during his final exam and setting up shape charges for precision blasts. He was top of his class at BUD/S and has been with the teams for three years, proving himself time and time again during field operations under fire. He's young, and yet he's the best EOD operator we have."

"Everyone starts somewhere, Master Chief. Anyone else?"

"Petty Officer 2nd Class Terry Jones is our sniper. Jones was born and raised near Omaha, Nebraska, where his father was a SWAT sniper for the city. His father taught him how to shoot when he was a boy, and he won several shooting competitions throughout his youth, including the 2017 national championship for the longest shot in his age bracket. Two thousand yards, to be precise."

Clint gave a low whistle and Paul continued. "After high school Jones enlisted in the Navy, because he was such a fan of *American Sniper*. He completed BUD/S and entered sniper school, where he graduated top of his class. His instructor said he hadn't seen someone with such raw talent since Chris Kyle himself. He's only been with the teams a short time, but Jones was the sniper on the same helicopter rescue mission with Wise and Barnes. Even though he's young, we couldn't have a better person protecting our team from above, sir."

Clint stood up. "Great lineup as always, Master Chief. I received a call from Jones's instructor before he was assigned to us, telling me how good he is. Let's go brief the men on what we have in store for them, shall we?"

As Clint and Paul walked into the room, the team came to attention. "Sir, let me introduce you to our team. This is Lieutenant Tom Wise (OIC); Senior Chief Bill Barnes (Platoon Chief); Chief Brent Norton (Communications); Chief Ryan Nolan (Advanced Special Operations); Petty Officer 1st Class Brian Beachier (Explosive Ordnance Disposal); and Petty Officer 2nd Class Terry Jones (Sniper)."

"At ease, men," Clint said, waving an arm at them. "Damn glad to meet you all. Some of you I know already, and the rest I will get to know before long. You've all been picked for this mission because you're the best in your particular skillset, and top notch excellence is required to conduct this operation. I'm proud to have each and every one of you on this mission.

"Now, LISTEN UP! We're to be inserted into hostile territory just outside the city of Wuhan, China. This operation's goal is the extraction of a Doctor Chin Lee

Shun. Dr. Shun is China's leading expert regarding the ability to weaponize viruses for biological warfare. We have reliable intel that shows Dr. Shun is ready to defect and expose his government's actions to the world. Our job is to go in undetected, join up with our CIA contact, extract Doctor Shun and escort him safely back to the States. Master Chief and I will go with you to set up command control. This mission is classified and personally authorized by POTUS. Go in, get the doc, and bring him back onto US soil. Is your mission perfectly clear?"

The team responded as one with a collective, "Yes, sir!"

"Master Chief Mitchell will discuss the details while we're in flight. Master Chief, load them up and let's get going ASAP."

Clint turned the briefing over to Paul and boarded the plane to discuss the flight plan with the pilots.

Once airborne, Paul laid out the details of the mission and assigned the team their responsibilities.

"All right, guys, gather round. We only have a three-hour window once we arrive in Wuhan to contact the CIA operative, confirm the location of Doctor Chin Lee Shun, make it out of Wuhan, and start heading back to the extraction point in Shanghai Harbor. We will have check-in points for updated intel as the mission progresses."

After a few hours in the air, the plane conducted

in-flight refueling operations just before it entered Senegal airspace.

Over the radio, the pilot said, "Commander Maxwell, we have just completed our first midair refueling on schedule. Next refuel will be near Diego Garcia Naval Base, and after that we will continue directly to Seoul."

"Affirmative, Lieutenant. Thanks for the update," acknowledged Clint over the radio.

"Master Chief, have you chatted with our CIA contact in Wuhan yet?"

"Not yet. So far I've only been in contact with the Hong Kong Operations Chief. We should receive that information once we land in Seoul, prior to boarding the submarine."

CHAPTER 4

Ride to Wuhan

THE PLANE CARRYING Clint and his team arrived in Seoul on schedule. A chief petty officer met them on the ground, popped a salute and said, "Commander Maxwell, I am Chief Torrance, and I will be driving you and your team over to Incheon to meet up with the USS Georgia."

Clint returned the salute. "Outstanding, Chief. If you don't mind, I'm going to have you coordinate our departure with Master Chief Mitchell."

Clint looked over his shoulder and shouted, "Master Chief! Chief Torrance will be our transportation to the sub."

"Yes, sir, I'll handle it."

The team loaded up on a bus to Incheon Harbor, where the USS Georgia submarine was serving as the command control platform for the mission. Captain Joe Smith revealed a small smile upon seeing Clint and

Paul. "Nice to see you again, Commander Maxwell, and you as well, Master Chief. Been a few months since we last spoke."

The three proceeded to the wardroom and briefed the officers and crew on what they were about to do. Joe began, "My crew has worked well with your team before, so I expect this mission to be no different. But I understand this time you and Master Chief will stay behind and run command and control from here, is that correct?"

"Affirmative, sir," replied Paul.

Once the mission was recapped and everyone understood their tasks, the team went to store their gear, eat, and get some rest before the seventy-two-hour transit to the insertion point.

* * *

Meanwhile, in Wuhan, CIA operative Chang Wu was relaxing in his apartment after finishing his dinner, when he received a secure message from the Hong Kong operations center. "Chang Wu, this is Station Chief Roberts, in Hong Kong. Contact me on a secure line, ASAP."

Wu went into his bedroom and, from under his bed, pulled out a box which contained a secure telephone, calling Station Chief Roberts. "This is 996 calling in to HKSC," stated Chang.

"Confirmed identity. This is a secure line. This is

Chief Roberts. Chang, I have an important assignment for you."

"Okay, Chief, what's the emergency?"

"I need you to travel to Shanghai and meet up with Commander Maxwell's team, take them to Wuhan, and connect Maxwell with Dr. Chin Lee Shun."

"I have people who can take care of that, Chief."

"Chang, you've been the CIA's point man for this since this whole situation went down. The director herself wants you to personally handle this assignment."

"I understand. I'll get started. The same code names as usual?"

"Crazy Horse and Sitting Bull, correct. Thanks, Chang."

Chang hung up the phone and sat back down in his chair. Knowing what he now did, he didn't want to leave Dr. Shun unprotected for even a moment, so he picked up his cell phone and called Wang Lu, a local crime lord who had often been able to make things happen when no one else could. "Wang Lu! This is Chang Wu. I need you to arrange to have a boat ready to pick up some cargo for me approximately two miles off the coast of Shanghai, and have the cargo taken to the rail yard for further transport to Wuhan."

"Of course, my friend, whatever you need. But what happens to your cargo once it reaches Wuhan?"

"Let me worry about that. Just let me know once everything is arranged. Oh, and one other thing. I need you to have a pinger installed on the boat to transmit 5 kHz at three-second intervals. Do you understand?"

"Yes. I will inform you once the arrangements have been made."

Chang sat down and typed out a message to Chief Roberts regarding his plan to extract Dr. Shun from Wuhan:

To: Station Chief Roberts
From: Chang Wu
Subject: Extract Plan

Chief, I will not leave Dr. Shun and risk losing him, so I have arranged for Commander Maxwell's team to be met approximately two miles off the coast of Shanghai by a fishing trawler and taken into port. A pinger will be installed at 5 kHz, transmitting at three-second intervals. This will be the vessel the team boards. Have Commander Maxwell's team ask to be taken to Crazy Horse. Once they have arrived at the harbor docks, they will be transported to the railyard in Shanghai and placed in a box car for their six-hour ride to Wuhan. I will meet them at the railyard and escort them to our safe house here in Wuhan and prepare to transfer custody of Dr. Shun to Commander Maxwell. Tell Maxwell my code name will be Crazy Horse, and his team must respond as Sitting Bull. This will serve as confirmation for our mission to move forward. Once Dr. Shun is in their custody, I will ensure they are safely transported back to Shanghai via the railyard, escorted to the dock, and taken out in a boat to meet up with the submarine for its return trip to Yokosuka, Japan. Once in Yokosuka, Dr. Shun and the team will be flown back to the United States to the CIA facility at Langley in McLean, VA. Please pass this to Commander Maxwell.

End of Message.

* * *

Back on the USS Georgia, after three days of the team idly working out, playing cards and watching movies, it was now 2300 hours on operation day and the SEAL team was mustered in the missile control room (MCC), waiting for their final briefing before departure. Capt. Smith provided the team with the latest intel about what to expect on the beach and any last-minute changes from CIA or 7th Fleet Command. Paul ensured the team was prepared and all their equipment checks were completed and ready to go.

"Commander Maxwell, I just received a message from Langley regarding your mission. I think you and Master Chief better have a look before we continue." Joe handed Clint the message.

Clint and Paul both read the communication from Chang Wu to Station Chief Roberts.

"Thanks for the heads-up, Joe. I was wondering when we would get that information. Listen up, guys, at 0300 hours..." Clint proceeded to relay Chang's instructions. "Remember, you are Sitting Bull and you need to be taken to see Crazy Horse. Once you've confirmed contact, you'll be transported to shore and then to a train heading to Wuhan. Once you arrive in Wuhan, you'll be met by Crazy Horse and taken to the CIA safe house there, to wait out daylight hours before you get the train back to Shanghai.

"Crazy Horse will ensure Dr. Shun is at the safe house for extraction. If there are any changes in plans, let us know via SATCOM so we can provide aid. Questions?"

Barnes said, "Crazy Horse? Sitting Bull? Hell, is the lieutenant General Custer?" The team broke out in laughter.

Clint shook his head. "If that's the only concern, then Master Chief, get the team ready to lock out."

"Yes, sir, Skipper," said Paul. "You all heard the commander. Get your asses to the lockout chamber and let's get ready to move out!"

Clint went with Joe up to the control room while the ship was preparing to go up to periscope depth. The control room was rigged for low-level white setting, in preparation for nighttime operations, to let everyone's eyes adjust to dimly lit screens. The captain ordered the fire-control tracking party to be stationed for the lockout operations, so extra personnel would be on hand to aid with whatever situation might occur.

"Captain has the conn," said Joe. "Officer of the Deck, status report."

"Captain, the fire-control tracking party is stationed. We've cleared our baffles and have several light craft and trawlers operating between three thousand and four thousand yards. It'll be tight, but nothing we haven't trained for."

"Very well, Officer of the Deck. Helm, all ahead one-third."

"Helm aye, maneuvering answers all ahead one-third, Captain."

"Very well, raising number two scope. Dive, take me to periscope depth."

"Take the ship to periscope depth," responded the Diving Officer of the Watch. "Dive, aye."

The ship proceeded up to periscope depth with no issues. After a safety sweep, the captain stated no close contacts, but spotted one craft at a distance. "Contact this bearing mark!" he said. "I believe this is a Shuke I class Chinese coastal patrol craft, range approximately eight thousand yards. Sonar, let me know if the vessel changes course and speed."

"Sonar, aye," said the sonar supervisor.

Joe continued to take several observations over the next several minutes, until it moved out of immediate range of the launch. "Chief of the Boat," he said, "Prepare to hover and launch the SDV (SEAL Delivery Vehicle).

"Aye, sir," said the Chief of the Boat. "Chief of the Watch, open the lockout chamber and have the team enter and secure themselves into the SDV."

"Aye, COB."

After a few minutes, the Chief of the Watch received confirmation that the team was in the lockout chamber and secured inside the SDV. "Request permission to flood down, equalize the DDS (Dry Dock Shelter), and prepare for launch."

"Very well, COB," replied the captain.

"Sir, the DDS is flooded down and equalized with external pressure. We are ready to open the outer door and launch the SDV."

"Very well, Chief of the Boat. Launch the SDV."

"Aye, sir. Chief of the Watch, launch the SDV."

The Chief of the Watch passed the orders to the lockout chamber. The outer door on the dry dock shelter was opened, and the driver of the SEAL delivery vehicle backed out and headed to the rendezvous point with the team. Clint and Paul were monitoring communications from the MCC. "So far so good," said Paul.

"Indeed," agreed Clint. "And now begins the waiting game."

*   *   *

Approximately twenty minutes later, the SDV driver said, "Lieutenant, the vessel located above us is emitting the 5 kHz transmitter at three-second intervals. This is your vessel, sir."

"Thanks, driver, we'll take it from here." Tom gave the order to detach from the SDV and prepare to board the vessel. He swam up to the boat and saw the pilot looking over the side. "I am Sitting Bull," he said. "Take me to Crazy Horse."

The boat pilot smiled. "I will take Sitting Bull to see Crazy Horse. I have been expecting you."

The pilot of the boat took the team to the dock, where a covered box truck was waiting to transport them to the railyard, just as expected.

Once the team arrived, the driver pulled up at the designated railcar and said, "Okay, we are here; you get out and board railcar now."

"Into the car!" shouted Tom.

The team crawled into a freight car that had been made ready for their six-hour journey to Wuhan.

"Chief Norton!" said Tom. "Pull out the SATCOM and inform Georgia of our current status. Let them know the operation is underway with no surprises so far."

"Yes sir, Lieutenant." Norton set up the SATCOM to report in. "Georgia, this is Sitting Bull. Stand by for update, over."

"Sitting Bull, this is Georgia. Standing by, over."

"Georgia, this is Sitting Bull. Team successfully boarded the transport vessel, arrived at dock, and safely transitioned to railcar. The operation is proceeding as planned. Acknowledge."

"Sitting Bull, this is Georgia, understand all, out."

Now all Clint and Paul could do was wait.

* * *

Back in Wuhan, Chang's cell phone rang. "Chang, this is Wang Lu. The cargo you requested made it safely to the railcar and is currently en route to Wuhan."

"Great news, Wang Lu! Thank you for getting my cargo on the train."

Chang hung up the phone and went back to sleep, knowing he would be up in a few hours to meet Dr. Shun and escort him to the safe house. So far everything was on schedule.

CHAPTER 5

Virus Creation

Several Months Earlier

D<small>R. C</small>HIN L<small>EE</small> Shun entered the front doors of the Wuhan Institute of Virology, which he headed. The primary purpose of the laboratory was to conduct scientific research on prevention and control of new infectious diseases in China through detection, research, and biosecurity prevention systems. Dr. Shun and his assistant, Dr. Wen Lu, entered the lab with the rest of Dr. Shun's team of virologists, to begin the morning briefing.

"Good morning, Doctor Shun!" said Dr. Lu.

"Good morning to you, Doctor Lu, and good morning to all of you. I suggest we get started. Today our team will be working on a variation of the SARS-CoV-2 coronavirus designated 'Project Airborne.'"

Dr. Lu took over. "This variant of the virus has the ability to read the DNA of the host environment it is exposed to. It can replicate itself and take advantage of the host's weaknesses, forcing the host's immune system into overdrive around a previously unknown condition, preventing it from fighting the virus itself."

"Doctor Lu and I made the discovery while analyzing the molecular structure of a coronavirus in horse bats," Shun continued. "We figured out how the virus could easily be transferred from bat to chimpanzee, and set up an experiment to test our thesis."

"Doctor Shun, this is an incredible discovery!" shouted one of the virologists. He turned to Dr. Phen, the leading virologist of the lab and a trusted friend of Shun. "Doctor Phen, if we can figure out how each of the unique coronaviruses could spread from animal to animal, perhaps we can figure out a way to eradicate it before it becomes a concern in human hosts?"

"Doctor Shun," Phen replied, "you theorized that if we could manipulate the genome of the virus, it would be possible for it to spread to humans and animals. Am I summarizing you correctly?"

"Yes, that's correct."

Dr. Phen continued, "Viral genomes are the fastest developing entities in biology, mainly because of their short replication time and enormous quantity of offspring. By recombining the host with other organisms, we should be successful in creating Project Airborne."

"Does anyone have any questions?" Shun asked.

When he was met with silence, he said, "Very well then, let's begin."

The team went through the strict testing protocols that Dr. Shun and Dr. Lu had provided for Dr. Phen and his virologists to create Project Airborne. By mid-morning, Phen called them back to the lab. He was filled with excitement and shouted as they entered, "My team of virologists and I have finished creating the genome for Project Airborne per your directions. Please have a look in the microscope. It worked! Your theories were correct! We can manipulate and control it."

Dr. Shun's heart was filled with excitement, so he was first to look at the new genome through the microscope. "I can't believe it, Doctor Lu! Our theories were correct. Now, if we can just figure out a way to transfer from host to host . . ."

"What's wrong, Doctor Shun? You appear to not be as happy after seeing our creation as you were hearing about it."

Dr. Shun stood up, grabbed Dr. Lu by the arm, and pulled him over to talk in a more private space. "Doctor Lu, do you realize that we have actually created a potential biological weapon?"

Dr. Lu's voice was firm as he said, "Doctor Shun, what did you think we were trying to achieve here? This has been our mission from the beginning."

Dr. Shun looked at his colleague. "Yes, my friend, but I didn't think we would actually accomplish it."

"We need to move into Phase II and start exposing the virus to hosts in order to determine in a controlled environment what it will actually do."

"You're right, Doctor Lu. Doctor Phen, tell your team to start preparations for animal testing."

"Right away, Doctor Shun. We will get started after lunch."

* * *

Ten days later, Dr. Phen paged Dr. Shun to the lab. "Doctor Shun," he said, "we are starting to see signs that the virus has infected the host. Congratulations! It appears we have a successful test!"

"This is good news, Doctor Phen. I am happy to see that our genome works. Now we need to conduct this test on other hosts and see if we can predict similar results."

Dr. Phen's team set up several more testing chambers and exposed hosts to the virus. Another ten days went by, and the hosts started showing symptoms. Dr. Phen called Shun and Lu back to the lab.

"Doctor Shun and Doctor Lu, I have exciting news. The genome we created has infected every host we exposed it to."

"That's wonderful news," replied Lu. "Unfortunately,

though," Phen said, "that is the only thing that went as expected."

"What do you mean?" inquired Shun.

"The virus did not interact the same way with all hosts. Each had similar symptoms, but different outcomes. Some got a severe cold and upper respiratory infection while others presented with influenza and pneumonia type symptoms—fever, body aches, and difficulty breathing. Doctor Shun, I would like to monitor these hosts for the next four weeks and only treat a few with antibiotics, to see if it can be controlled."

"All right, Doctor Phen, let's see what happens once the virus reaches maturity in the hosts."

After the four-week period was over, Shun and Lu went back to Phen's lab to hear the results. "All hosts showed signs of physical exhaustion for two to four weeks," Phen announced. "The treatment that provided the best results was hydroxychloroquine. Other antibiotics had no effect. The critically ill hosts who were not administered hydroxychloroquine, died."

"Doctor Phen and Doctor Lu," replied Shun, "please meet me in the main conference room in one hour to continue our discussion regarding Project Airborne." Shun went back to his office and shut his door. He couldn't get the test results out of his head.

An hour later, they resumed their discussion. "Neither of you know this, but these test results were very disturbing to me. We have created a potential biological weapon that, based on our testing, can spread so rapidly it would overwhelm medical facilities and shut down any country's economy until a cure could be created. The takeover of an entire country could occur without firing a single shot."

"Doctor Shun, I'm confused," said Phen. "Our objective for the Ministry of Health was precisely to accomplish this. We all knew that if we were successful, Doctor Lee would have us figure out how to prep the virus on a warhead or similar device to deploy as the military's next bioweapon. Are you having second thoughts?"

"Doctors, we must look at this from an ethical and moral point of view. Do we really want to unleash something like this on other human beings?"

"Doctor Shun," said Lu, "I know you have been under a lot of stress lately, with Doctor Lee constantly hounding you about results, but we have finished our work on Project Airborne. As far as I am concerned, we can send the results to Doctor Lee and start on our next project for the Ministry of Health."

"I am in firm agreement with Doctor Lu," added Phen. "We have completed our mission, and now we must move on to the next project."

"If that's how you both feel, I will prepare the report and send it to Doctor Lee."

But for several days after the completion of the original experiments, Dr. Shun wrestled with whether or not to send the results of his experiments to the Ministry of Health. Ultimately, he prepared the report and delivered it to Doctor Wong Chen Lee.

CHAPTER 6

The Virus is Released!

D R. LEE WAS the head of the Ministry of Health. He oversaw all projects related to military use from defense-sponsored facilities. A tall, slender man, physically fit for a person in his mid-fifties, he was a brilliant virologist who enjoyed the political scene and the power it afforded him. He was sitting in his office, reviewing reports, when Dr. Suyin entered.

"Doctor Lee! Our monitoring of the Wuhan lab has paid dividends. Doctor Lu just notified me they had a major breakthrough in the realm of virus genome manipulation; a new strain that has the potential of being weaponized."

"If this is true, Doctor Suyin, I do not intend to wait here for the report. Make arrangements for you, Doctor Zhang, and me to travel down to Wuhan and look at the data first-hand."

"Yes, sir. I will make all the necessary arrangements."

*   *   *

Meanwhile, back at the lab in Wuhan . . . "Doctor Shun, Doctor Suyin just informed me that she, Doctor Lee, and Doctor Zhang will be traveling down to Wuhan tomorrow, to go over our results from Project Airborne."

"Very well, then. Doctor Lu, prepare the conference room and have Doctor Phen ensure that all the relevant data is assembled for our visitors to review."

Dr. Shun was deeply disturbed at the thought that their recent discovery would not help humanity, but instead might help destroy it. This was the decisive moment when he knew he had to do something rash.

Lee and his colleagues, Zhang and Suyin, arrived in Wuhan the following day and stayed at the Hyatt Regency on Luohu Road. They met Dr. Shun and his team in the primary conference room at the lab the next morning.

"Good morning, Dr. Shun," said Dr. Lee. "I'm excited to review the results of your experiments regarding Project Airborne."

"I have provided our results in the reports on the table," said Shun. "My team and I are standing by to answer any of your questions."

"Thank you for your assistance, Doctor Shun, but we will not require any further assistance. Please leave the room and allow us to get to work."

Dr. Lee and his colleagues sifted through data for

the next couple of hours. Afterwards, he said to this team, "The results of the studies on the animal hosts are fascinating. I think Project Airborne has terrific potential."

"Absolutely, Doctor Lee. No doubt about it" replied Suyin.

"It appears that Doctor Shun and his team have done what we requested," said Zhang. "They have created Project Airborne."

Dr. Lee picked up the phone and called Dr. Shun's office. "Doctor Shun, please report with your team to the conference room for a debriefing."

"Understood, Doctor Lee. We are on our way." Shun hung up the phone and stopped by Lu and Phen's offices on his way to the meeting.

"How may we assist your team, Doctor Lee?"

"The results I have seen from your animal experiments are impressive. Have you thought of testing this on a human host?"

"Why would we expose this to a human host? This study was only intended to test animal-to-animal exposure, not animal-to-human or even human-to-human."

"Doctor Shun, you do realize this has the highest probability of being a biological weapon for our government? Your task was to create Project Airborne and be able to provide a means to deploy it if necessary," snapped Dr. Lee.

"Our directive did not include a means to deploy the virus. We were only tasked to create it."

"That is not the answer I was looking for. So, let me inform you what will happen next. We will take over the next phase of testing, to include human hosts."

"I cannot believe what I'm hearing," shouted Shun. "You want to conduct human host testing of the Project Airborne virus?!"

"Indeed. As a matter of fact, we will need some volunteers to be our guinea pigs." Dr. Lee sat back in his chair and looked at Dr. Shun. "Do not worry, Doctor. We will pay them for their cooperation and their silence."

Dr. Shun knew that if these tests were successful, the plan to weaponize Project Airborne was almost certain.

Dr. Lee stood up and addressed the room, "Attention, everyone. We will be taking over the next phase of testing regarding Project Airborne. Doctor Shun's team has agreed to assist us where necessary."

"Doctor Lee," said Zhang, "I have a colleague over at the local prison who can help us with volunteers."

"Make the call, Doctor Zhang. Doctor Lu, I need you to assist Doctor Zhang with the logistics."

"Yes, Doctor Lee."

And so it began. Dr. Lee's colleagues had a group of human volunteers brought in from the local prison to be their guinea pigs. They started slowly at first, only exposing one person and monitoring the effects. After seven days, the first human host started showing symptoms.

Dr. Lee was beside himself with excitement. He ordered another human host placed in the same room, to see if the virus would transfer. After an hour of exposure, they isolated the second host in a separate room. Approximately seven days later, the second human started showing symptoms similar to the first. Lee knew now that he had a biological weapon to boost his government's warfare capabilities.

"Doctor Phen, have the remaining volunteers exposed by various methods and time periods to determine the behavior patterns of the virus."

"Right away, Doctor."

*   *   *

A few weeks went by while testing was in progress. After implementing various methods of transference and exposure times, the team had learned the full capability of the virus.

"Doctors Suyin and Zhang," said Lee, "gather all the data associated with Project Airborne and prepare to head back to Beijing. Doctor Shun, you and your team have done some monumental work here. Your government thanks you for your service."

"Doctor Lee, would you like for me to work on a cure for the new virus in case we ever need it?"

"Absolutely not! You will take all the infected patients back to the prison to have them destroyed and incinerated."

"What?! Doctor Lee, I must protest! We cannot have patients destroyed. They are human beings! Let me work on a cure, so I can send them back to the prison healthy."

Dr. Lee was getting agitated. "Doctor Shun, I acknowledge your protest. Now, understand what I am about to tell you. You will take all of the infected patients back to the prison, have them destroyed, and their bodies burned. Do I make myself clear?"

"Yes, Doctor Lee, you have made yourself perfectly clear."

Dr. Lee and his colleagues left the lab in Wuhan and headed back to Beijing with all the Project Airborne data, or so they thought. Secretly, before they left, Shun made a private copy of the material for himself. He gathered Phen and Lu in his office. "Are we sure that hydroxychloroquine will work on humans, since we never had the opportunity to test it?"

"We have no idea if it will work on humans, but I would safely assume it would," replied Phen.

"I would agree with that assessment," said Lu.

"Doctor Phen, let's try a dose of hydroxychloroquine on one of the sickest prisoners, to see if he responds to the drug as well as the infected animals did."

Unfortunately, Dr. Lee had already thought of that

and ordered a special military security detachment from the nearby army command center to take custody of the prisoners. Captain Lee Wong was in charge of the detail, a highly decorated officer and a true Chinese patriot who followed the orders of his superiors without question.

Dr. Lee met Captain Wong at the primary entrance to the lab before he headed back to Beijing. "Captain Wong," he said, "do not let anyone from this facility deter you. In fact, I am the only one who can change your current orders. Is that clear?"

"Crystal clear, sir."

Captain Wong turned to his sergeant and said, "Sergeant! Have the men dressed in hazmat suits so we can take custody of the remaining sick prisoners."

"Yes, sir. I will take care of it."

Captain Wong entered the lab where Doctors Shun, Lu, and Phen were discussing a possible treatment for the virus. "Doctor Shun," he said, "I am Captain Wong. I have been assigned by Dr. Lee to take custody of the remaining infected prisoners."

The doctors were a little disturbed by a military officer coming into the facility, but they took him to the prisoners. The soldiers escorted the prisoners to the loading dock, where a two-ton cargo box truck was standing by to transport them back to the prison.

The truck had three benches for the prisoners to sit on during transit, fitting twelve altogether. The incinerator they were being taken to was approximately twenty-five kilometers from the lab, so it would take them a little over thirty minutes in Wuhan traffic to get there.

Approximately ten kilometers from the incinerator, they were passing through an intersection when another vehicle ran the light and hit the truck so hard on its right side that it rolled over onto its left side. The driver and passenger in the transport truck were knocked unconscious. The escort vehicle was too far ahead and didn't see the accident occur, so did not stop, and kept heading toward its destination.

Captain Wong and two of his men were following a couple hundred yards behind when the truck was struck by the other vehicle. Captain Wong immediately raced up to the rolled-over truck and tried to control the people coming towards it. "Stay away from this truck!" he shouted. "It is carrying hazardous material and is a danger to you and the environment. Please, do not approach this vehicle."

The driver and passenger were pulled from the cab safely and taken to a local hospital. The back door of the truck had popped open during the crash, and two of the prisoners were ejected and lying in the street. Folks ran over to help them just as Captain Wong drove up. One spectator was a doctor and started treating the two prisoners in the street.

"Someone check the back of the truck to see if anyone else is in there!" shouted the doctor. "I will start treating these two men. Someone please call for help! We will need to get these two to the closest hospital. They're in pretty bad shape."

Captain Wong was furious that the doctor had treated his prisoners. "What are you doing over there? I told everyone to move away from the truck."

"I am a doctor, I must assist the injured people. You need to help remove the others from the truck so I can assess their condition and if needed, have them transported to the hospital."

Captain Wong knew he had to put a stop to all of this in a hurry, or the situation would get out of hand. "Sergeant!" he yelled. "Grab some gas from the vehicle and set fire to the truck. Throw the two prisoners back in and lock the door."

"Yes, sir."

The doctor was stunned and horrified at what he was hearing. "What the hell are you doing?!" he yelled. "You cannot set the truck on fire. There are still people trapped inside!"

"I told you to back away from the truck, Doctor, but you did not. So now you will meet the same fate as your patients." The captain pulled out his sidearm and shot the doctor.

"Sergeant! Shoot the remaining prisoners."

"Yes, sir,"

What Captain Wong didn't realize, though, was that several people had started helping prisoners out of the wrecked truck. A number of them had run off before he could see or catch them.

Captain Wong and his team continued to watch the truck burn when the police and fire department arrived. "What the hell is going on here?" asked the police chief.

"The truck was filled with hazardous and classified material, so I need your help, Chief, to keep everyone away until it has burned itself out."

Both the police and fire chief, knowing who Captain Wong was, reluctantly agreed to his request.

It did not take long before the news of what had happened reached the Wuhan laboratory.

"Doctor Shun!" said the head of security. "I've just received word over the police radio of a major accident just up the road from here. It appears a truck caught fire, and all of the people inside the truck were killed."

"Thank you for the news, officer. Let's hope Captain Wong's detail was not involved in the accident."

In his own mind, he knew that the virus had just been released on the public of Wuhan, and that there would be a serious pandemic ahead of them if he did not work on a cure. Shun notified Dr. Lee of what had happened, but he did not show any empathy towards the situation.

"Doctor Shun, you will not speak of this matter to anyone. You will not acknowledge that we were at your facility, or what you discovered, or that you were ever involved with Project Airborne. Do you understand?"

Shun answered, "I understand that you are trying to protect your recent discovery, Doctor Lee, but do you realize the implications now that they have exposed the virus to other humans? If you do not let me work on a cure, you will surely have a situation here that will completely get out of control within a few weeks, and you will not be able to stop it for quite some time."

"Doctor Shun, I will tell you once again, you officially have no knowledge of this project, nor knowledge of an accident today, nor of anything related to this matter. From now on you will say publicly only that you continue to work with the Ministry of Health on various infectious diseases and viruses. Got it?

"I understand." Shun left the laboratory and headed home, to think about today's events and what might happen next.

CHAPTER 7

The Outbreak!

S EVERAL MONTHS PRIOR to the arrival of
Commander Maxwell's team in Wuhan, the news
of what had occurred on the streets of that city
spread quickly to informants of the CIA in Hong Kong.

Station Chief Roberts called Chang with urgency.
"I need you to reach out to your network and find out
what the hell happened in Wuhan, then get back to me
ASAP."

"Well, nice to hear your voice, Chief! Yes, I'm fine.
Thanks for asking."

"Chang, I don't have time to go into pleasantries
here. I need you to figure this out. We're hearing that
something big has happened, and we need to know
what it is."

"All right, Chief. I'll reach out to some of my associates
here and figure out what's going on."

"Godspeed, Chang. Roberts out."

Chang picked up his cell phone and called Chen,

his trusted associate within the Wuhan criminal underworld. "Chen, I need you to ask around and find out what happened in Wuhan this afternoon. Get back to me ASAP!"

"Yes, boss, I'll make some inquiries. I heard that the military was involved with some sort of hazardous chemical spill, but I will dig deeper."

Chen reached out to his network of folks in Wuhan and, after a few hours, figured out exactly what had taken place. Chang's cell phone rang. "This is Chang."

"Chang, this is Chen. I know what happened in Wuhan this afternoon."

"Well, I'm waiting."

"Sorry, boss. It appears that a two-ton box truck was carrying prisoners from the Wuhan lab back to the prison, escorted by the military. Not exactly sure why, but I hope to find that out soon. The truck was involved in an accident at an intersection. Several people jumped in to help the men in the truck, including a doctor who was having a meal at a nearby cafe. Once the military escort showed up, the officer in charge ordered the prisoners shot and set the truck on fire. The name of the escort's captain was Wong, from the nearby Army base. Wong argued with the doctor, who ignored orders to stop. Wong pulled out his pistol and shot the doctor. Once the police and fire chiefs arrived, they spoke to Wong and continued to do his bidding. That's all that I have for you, boss."

"Were you able to find out why the military was so protective of the prisoners only to have them shot and burned?" Chang asked.

"Yes and no. I was informed by a very reliable source at the lab regarding the prisoners, but I am not sure I believe it."

"Tell me, Chen, and let me figure out if it is factual or not."

"Well, my contact said the prisoners on that truck were subjected to a lot of tests in the lab regarding a virus, some type of Top-Secret classified project Doctor Shun was working on, called Project Airborne. Sounds a little fishy to me, but I would say that whatever it is they were testing on those prisoners won't be discussed on the evening news."

"Thanks, Chen. I'll be in touch. See if you can track down Doctor Shun."

Chang knew he had a potential outbreak of an infectious disease that had inadvertently been released on the citizens of Wuhan. He picked up the phone and got Station Chief Roberts updated with the information. A few hours later, he received a call back from Chen. "I know where you can find Dr. Shun this evening. He has dinner every evening at a small restaurant named Lulu's on his way home from the lab."

"Thanks for the information, Chen. I'll take it from here."

Later that evening, Chang made sure he was at Lulu's

when Dr. Shun arrived. The doctor sat alone at his usual table in the back corner, where he could see everyone. He ordered his usual Friday evening meal of sweet and sour chicken with sticky rice. Once he started eating, Chang came over and sat down at his table, bowing first, out of respect. "Hello, Doctor. My name is Chang. It is a pleasure to meet you, sir."

Shun stopped eating. "I'm sorry, have we met before?"

"No, Doctor, but I think I can help you with a problem you have at the lab."

"I don't know who you are, but I assure you I do not have any problem at the lab."

"Oh, I'm sorry, I must have you mixed up with another Doctor Shun who worked on Project Airborne and inadvertently released it to the citizens of Wuhan. My mistake."

Shun dropped his chopsticks with a look of horror on his face. "WHO ARE YOU? How do you know about that? That project is highly classified. Do you know what could happen to you for uttering those words?"

"Well, yes, I do, Doctor. If the government finds out what truly happened here, they will attempt to get rid of any evidence that would suggest they had anything to do with it, then make up some fake press announcement regarding animal-to-human transfer at an exotic market. So, you have a choice: you can work with me, and I can ensure you have safe passage to the United States, where you can address what happened here today and hold the people accountable for their actions, or you can do nothing and risk being disposed of with the rest of the evidence. Are you interested in my proposal, Doctor?"

Shun sat there in complete amazement. After a minute of silent consideration, he picked up his chopsticks and continued eating, saying, "I am not sure who you are or how you learned about this nonsense, but you had better leave me alone and go about your business before I report you to the authorities."

Chang smiled at Dr. Shun and placed a business card on the table in front of him. "Call me if you reconsider. I will be glad to meet you here for dinner another time."

Shun picked up Chang's business card and placed it in his pocket. Chang stood up and walked out of the restaurant to head home. Chang wasn't worried; he knew it would take several weeks before Dr. Shun would discover his life was truly in danger. He was confident that before long, the doctor would come and seek his help.

CHAPTER 8

Dr. Shun's Nightmare

I T HAD BEEN several months since Chang met Dr. Shun at Lulu's for dinner. Shun was beginning to get concerned regarding the sickness that had engulfed the city of Wuhan, and how the military had stepped in to control the outbreak. Everything Chang told him had started coming true, down to every last detail.

Shun was feeling paranoid and uneasy—always looking around corners, opening bathroom stalls, surveilling restaurants before he sat down to eat, and even setting up a security camera system in his apartment. One day, while he was driving over to eat at Lulu's, he suspected he was being followed by an unmarked car. He continued to the restaurant, parked his car, entered Lulu's, and sat at his usual table in the back corner. He ordered his dinner.

Just after Shun entered the restaurant, two very well-dressed men entered behind him and ordered food at the front.

Dr. Shun continued to watch the two men eat their meals at the front of the restaurant. Occasionally, one of them would glance back at him. This made him feel especially uneasy, and the ideas Chang had put into his head started running through his thoughts.

No longer hungry, Shun paid his bill and left the restaurant, deliberately avoiding eye contact with the two men as he passed them on his way out. He hoped he was just overthinking everything.

Once outside and in his car, Dr. Shun noticed the two men from the front of the restaurant exit and look around to see where he had gone. This confirmed his worst fears—he was being followed—*but why?* He had said nothing to anyone about the incident four months ago. *What did they want?* Lots of things passed through his mind. Maybe Chang was right; they would clean up any evidence that might implicate the government, and even cover up the release of a virus to the public. Or was Chang trying to intimidate him?

Dr. Shun started his car, drove home, and turned on the news. What he saw next was alarming. The reporter was saying, "I am down by the fish market, where the virus started. As of today, people are showing signs of influenza or pneumonia at an alarming rate. Our hospitals are filling up, and we are running out of resources to effectively contain this. The government is sending in soldiers to assist the police chief here with enforcing a stay-inside curfew for the next several days. I am not sure how long these curfews will last, so I may be reporting from here for a while." Shun knew right away that this was his virus at work. He started sweating; his palms were clammy and his brain was on overload. He started to panic. He knew he was being watched by the government. How long would they let him live? What could he do now? He reached in his coat pocket, and there was Chang's business card. He picked up the phone and called. "Chang, Dr. Shun here. I would like to invite you to dinner at Lulu's next Friday night. Are you free?"

"I believe I can make it, Doctor. Let's say 7:00 if that's okay with you?"

"Looking forward to it. I will see you next Friday." Shun hung up the phone.

*   *   *

Chang and Chen arrived at the restaurant Friday evening on schedule.

"Chen, I want your men placed around the diner for security, in case we need to extract Doctor Shun at once."

"I have my men stationed in various locations. The area is secure."

"Thank you. I will let you know if I require any more assistance tonight."

At the appointed hour, Chang once again entered

the restaurant and sat down at Dr. Shun's table. "Good evening, Doctor! How is the food tonight?"

"Tonight's special is kung pao chicken. One of my favorite dishes."

"That sounds delightful. I think I will order the same thing."

Chang called over to the waiter, "I will have the same thing he is having, with a glass of water, please."

"Yes, sir, I will bring it right out for you."

Chang looked at Dr. Shun and said, "Have you been watching the news, Doctor?"

"Why yes, I have. It has been quite alarming. I am glad that I don't live down by the market."

"Oh, it will get worse, or at least that's what I'm hearing. Doctor, do you realize that your virus has not just infected the citizens of Wuhan, but there are reports from all over the world of people coming down with similar symptoms?"

Doctor Shun stared at Chang in disbelief. His mouth had involuntarily dropped open. "People all over the world are coming down with similar symptoms as the virus here?"

"That's correct, Doc. Your virus is spreading at an alarming rate."

Chang's meal arrived, and he proceeded to eat while Shun sat there staring at him. "Why are you staring at me, Doctor?" he said with a smile. "Please, eat your food before it gets cold. You were right; this is really good." Once finished, Chang wiped his mouth with a napkin and said, "So, Doc, are you starting to get a little paranoid that your virus is making people around the world sick?"

"Why yes, actually. I have been noticing two gentlemen monitoring my coming and goings lately, and I am getting worried. I had no idea the virus had spread outside of Wuhan. The news has not reported anything outside of Wuhan to the public."

"Well, of course not, Doc. The government would never allow foreign news agencies to cover this event. They don't want the citizens of Wuhan or the rest of the Chinese people to know this is a worldwide event now. However, I can help you with the two men following you. All you have to do is say, 'What do you want me to do now, Mr. Chang?'"

Shun paused and thought about what he should say next, and quickly realized he had no choice. "What do you want me to do now, Mr. Chang?"

"Doc, we need you to go back to your lab next week and retrieve all the information you need to prove your case. Meet me back here next Friday night for dinner. Do you understand?"

"Yes, I understand."

Chang got up from the table and left. Once home, he got on his secure phone and informed his station chief that he had made the deal and needed an extraction for next Friday evening.

Dr. Shun stayed in his apartment all weekend, worried about what might happen to him. Now and then he looked out his window. There was an unmarked black sedan sitting in front of his building. Someone was watching him. Was it Doctor Lee, or was Chang watching him?

Monday morning came, and he proceeded to the lab as usual. His two new friends followed him from the time he stepped into his car until he arrived in the parking garage at the lab. This game of cat and mouse continued over the next few days. That Friday, Dr. Shun arrived at the lab at his normal time and worked in his office for most of the morning. He attended a couple of meetings after lunch with Dr. Lu, then retreated to his office. He had been gathering all the information he needed on a flash drive he kept in a safe. He retrieved the flash drive, placed it in his pocket, and closed out his final day at the lab. He was in his car and just about to leave the premises when security stopped him.

"Doctor Shun! You left your umbrella by the front desk," said the security officer.

Shun's mind raced. *What did I do? Why are you bothering me? I am on my way home. What is it?* All kinds of things rushed through his mind. "Thank you, Officer. I have a lot on my mind these days."

"That's okay, Doc. Don't want you to get wet on your way home."

"Thanks again, Officer. Goodnight." After that near-meltdown of his nervous system, Shun went home to get ready for his dinner with Chang.

CHAPTER 9

The Extraction

THE TRAIN TRANSPORTING the extraction team arrived at the railyard in Wuhan at 11:00 a.m. Chang found the railcar the team was in and established contact. "This is Crazy Horse, and I am about to engage hostiles at Little Bighorn."

Lt. Wise replied, "This is Sitting Bull. I am on your flank and ready to engage."

Chang opened the railcar door. "Hello, everyone, my name is Chang, and I will be your CIA contact for your stay here in Wuhan. I bet you all had a splendid ride all the way from Shanghai."

The team looked at him and shook their heads. "We've had worse."

"Senior Chief Barnes, notify Command that we've met up with Crazy Horse and the mission is proceeding as planned," ordered Tom.

Bill broke out the SATCOM and established comms to provide their sitrep.

Clint and Paul had to be patient and wait. Their team's fate was in the CIA's hands for now.

"Lieutenant, get your team and load up the truck. I'll be taking you to one of our CIA safe houses while I go meet Doctor Shun for dinner."

"You heard the man. Grab your gear and get in the truck!"

The truck left the railyard and disappeared into Wuhan traffic without incident. Later, at the warehouse that served as an isolated and secure safe house, the team unpacked their gear, got something to eat, and rested prior to their departure in about eight hours.

* * *

Chang arrived at Lulu's fifteen minutes early for his dinner with Dr. Shun. Before he ordered, he called Chen. "Is the security perimeter in place for tonight?"

"It is. I also have backup ready in case you need assistance."

"Thanks. I hope we won't be needing them. I will call you once we are ready to leave the restaurant." Chang ordered his food and patiently waited for Dr. Shun, but after fifteen minutes, Dr. Shun had not arrived. The doctor was a very punctual man, and this was an alarm to Chang. At first he thought that maybe the doctor had changed his mind, so he called Chen again. "Chen, I'm getting a little worried. Head over to his apartment, see if he's still there and report back to me."

* * *

An hour earlier, Shun arrived at his apartment complex at the usual time, parked his car in the garage, and went to his apartment. As he approached his door, he noticed it was cracked open. He knew something wasn't right, but he couldn't call the police without drawing attention to his work at the lab. He pushed open the door to find the two men who had been following him for the past couple of weeks, sitting at the kitchen table.

"Good evening, Doctor!" one of them said, standing. "I hope you had a wonderful day at work."

"Who are you guys? And why are you in my apartment? Why have you been following me?"

"Doc, don't get so upset. We just want you to tell us who you are meeting for dinner tonight. We know you're having second thoughts about what happened a few months ago at the lab."

Shun didn't know what to say at first, but eventually answered, "I always go to Lulu's for dinner; you know that already because you guys have been eating there along with me for the past couple of weeks! I always eat in the corner by myself, and you all always eat in the front and glance back at me! What is it you really want from me? Doctor Lee does not trust me or what?"

"Doc, you will be missing your dinner at Lulu's tonight. We are keeping you here until Captain Wong can come over and pick you up."

Shun knew at that moment that he was in real trouble, and he had no way of reaching out to Chang for help. Would Chang come over once he realized that something was wrong? Or would he just call the night a wash and try to reach out to him later? Lots of different scenarios were going through the doctor's mind.

"Doc, I suggest you sit down and relax until Captain Wong arrives. If you want to eat, I can have food brought in."

"What I really want is to go to Lulu's and have my normal Friday night dinner, but that doesn't seem possible at the moment." With nothing else to discuss, Shun moved into the living room and grabbed a book he had been reading earlier, sat down on his couch, and tried to relax. The other two men settled in the kitchen and waited on Captain Wong.

Chen arrived at Dr. Shun's apartment complex and found his car parked in its normal space in the parking garage. Nothing out of the ordinary so far.

As he conducted surveillance of the apartment, Chen noticed the two men sitting at Dr. Shun's kitchen table, smoking cigarettes, but Dr. Shun was nowhere to be seen, at least from Chen's current viewpoint. He moved around to the other side of the apartment, to another window where he could see into the living room, and there sat Shun on the couch, reading a book. He could tell that even though everything appeared normal, two men sitting at the kitchen table smoking while Dr. Shun sat in his living room reading, didn't add up.

He called Chang. "Boss, I am over at Dr. Shun's apartment. I believe two men are holding him here against his will."

"Thanks for the update, Chen. We cannot act on this without following protocol. I have to go through proper channels or it can come back to bite us. Call me the moment something changes." Chang gathered his things and headed to the safe house.

As he entered, he was met by an angry Lieutenant Wise, who shouted, "Where the hell have you been? We're behind schedule!"

"It appears the doctor's luck has run out," Chang replied in a serious tone, updating Wise on the situation.

"How far is the doctor's apartment from here?"

"Twenty minutes at this time of the evening. Why do you ask?"

"We came here to perform an extraction, and that's what we're going to do. Lieutenant, we need to get eyes on our target. Chief Nolan, go with Chang and let's get some surveillance on that apartment. Recon the area for a quiet way in and out, and report back on our unit comms link."

"Copy that, Senior Chief. Come on, Chang, move your ass."

When Ryan and Chang arrived and started scouting out the area, they learned that nothing had changed in the last hour. Chang called Chen to come meet them outside, and the three tried to figure out the quickest and quietest way to enter the apartment.

"Okay, Chang, this is how I see this going down," said Ryan. "You and I will remain in a position to supply cover fire here on top of the building, across the street, and on the south side of the apartment, if needed. Most important for this to happen fast and easy is real-time intel. The lieutenant and Senior Chief Barnes will approach the apartment from the south, enter the building on the first floor, and make their way up the stairs to the second floor, positioning themselves to the right of the apartment door. Chief Norton and Petty Officer Beachier will enter from the north side and continue up the stairs to the second floor, meeting the lieutenant and Senior Chief Barnes on the left-hand side of the apartment door.

"Petty Officer Jones will position himself on the west side facing the kitchen window of the apartment, and on my command will take out the two men sitting at the table. Once the threat is eliminated, the lieutenant, Senior Chief Barnes, Chief Norton, and Petty Officer Beachier will enter the apartment through the front door, secure the apartment, retrieve Dr. Shun, and exit the building on the south side to a truck that Chen will supply to transport us back to the safe house."

"Sounds like a solid plan to me," said Chang.

"Chen, tactfully place your men around a five-block radius from the apartment, blocking off any egress. No one gets within spitting distance of the apartment without us knowing about it. Also, we'll need a second truck to conceal our escape, positioned on the south side of the building."

"I'm on it, Chief."

Ryan looked at Chang and said, "Now we wait and see what happens. I want to ensure nothing surprises us. Position yourself here on the edge of the roof and watch the street while I report our findings to the lieutenant and Senior Chief."

Ryan contacted Tom and Bill and provided all the information they had gathered, along with the assault plan to breach the apartment and extract Dr. Shun.

Everyone knew the plan; each person had his role to play.

"Chief, the plan is solid," acknowledged Tom. "I still think it's risky, but our orders were clear: extract Dr. Shun."

"Senior Chief, get on SATCOM and update Georgia on our situation."

"I'm on it, sir," he replied, as he set up to discuss the plan with Clint and Paul. "Georgia, this is Sitting Bull. Stand by for sitrep. Over."

"Sitting Bull, this is Georgia. Standing by. Go ahead."

"Situation on the ground has changed. Target being detained; team preparing to extract. Over."

"Sitting Bull, this is Georgia. Understand sitrep. You're on your own. Godspeed. Georgia out."

Clint was not happy about the change, but no operation ever went as planned. The risk of capture had just gone up considerably, and there was no way to get any support from the outside, so far deep inside hostile territory. The team would be on their own. Now all Clint and Paul could do was wait.

The rest of the team left the safe house and went over to the staging area one block from the apartment. They were making their way to the kickoff point when three vehicles, one truck and two sedans, breached Chen's security perimeter. He called Chang to let him know and Chang updated the others.

"Chief," Chang said. "We have company."

"I see them." Ryan grabbed his comm link and said, "Potential hostiles coming in from the west. One truck and two sedans. Hold fast."

The team stopped, waiting for further instructions as the vehicles pulled up on the south side of the building. Ryan was looking through his binoculars and saw a military officer get out of the first car— Captain Wong. Wong had six men with him, and they all headed up to Dr. Shun's apartment.

Ryan clicked his comm link. "Looks like we have seven more people who want to join our party."

"Roger. Keep us posted on their location. Are we clear to enter the building?"

"Negative. I'll let you know once they have entered."
Now the plan had to change. The team would have to
clear the room.

Ryan was already developing a scheme to breach the
apartment. He grabbed his comm link and said, "Jones,
I need you to position yourself so you have eyes on the
apartment and a clear line of fire. Move now."

"I'm on it."

"Lieutenant, have Beachier assume the breacher role
and place explosives on the door, then position himself
behind Barnes, who will lead the first advance into the
room. Immediately before entering, Norton will throw
stun grenades to cause confusion. The team will enter
and eliminate all hostiles, secure the room, and take Dr.
Shun into custody. Any questions?"

"Sounds good, Chief. Just let us know when to
execute."

"No time to update Command on our recent
development. We're on our own."

"No worries. We have Nolan on the rooftop. No one
better than him to make this call right now."

"I hope you're right."

Captain Wong and his men entered the apartment
building. Ryan clicked on his comm link. "Jones, inform
me once you have eyes on targets and you are ready to
fire."

"I have eyes on them right now. Standing by to
execute on your orders."

"Lieutenant, our guests have entered the apartment. Proceed to the front door and prepare to breach."

"Understood. Moving out now."

Captain Wong walked into the apartment along with his men. "Hello again, Doctor! It has been a while since we spoke last. Dr. Lee has instructed me to take you to Beijing for further debriefing."

"Do you expect me to believe that?" replied Dr. Shun.

"I don't care what you think, Doctor, but you are coming with me. Arrest the good doctor and prepare to move out!"

The team was climbing the stairs and preparing to conduct the breach when, out of nowhere, a bright light filled the living room of Dr. Shun's apartment. Ryan could see something was going on. "Jones, can you see anything from your vantage point?"

"All I see is a bright ball of light. Wait a minute— there appears to be something coming out of the ball of light . . . holy shit! There's something strange going on in there."

Noise from the flash grenades was heard as the team approached the door. "It appears something incapacitated our guests," said Terry.

"What do you mean, incapacitated? What the hell are you talking about?"

Ryan was now able to see into the apartment, where he glimpsed a bright light in the living room with what appeared to be two additional men scurrying around. Ryan could not believe what he was seeing!

"Dammit, Chief, what the hell is going on?" shouted Tom.

"Sir, I really have no words to describe it."

"Chief, we're going in. Breach now," ordered Tom.

As the team entered the room, what they saw next was something out of a science fiction movie. An enormous round ball of energy in the form of a tunnel was in the middle of the room, with two men preparing to go through it. A quick scan of the room showed that Captain Wong and his six men, plus the original two men, were unconscious, along with Dr. Shun, lying sideways on the couch. Tom and Bill both got a quick look at the two men near the ball of light, who to their amazement looked just like . . .

The two men stepped into the ball of light and it disappeared. The team was left standing in Dr. Shun's apartment with seven unconscious Chinese soldiers, two plain-clothes security officers, and Dr. Shun. They had no idea what had just taken place, but they had to continue with the mission.

"What the hell was that, Lieutenant?" asked Senior Chief Barnes.

"Later, Senior Chief. We have to grab Dr. Shun and get the hell out of here before anybody else pops in on us tonight!"

The team made their way down the stairs and out to the truck that Chen had provided for their escape. Ryan and Terry both left their positions and were making their way down to the truck to join the rest of the team. Chang left his position and hooked up with Chen, and the two headed back to the safe house to meet the others.

"You guys aren't gonna believe what I just saw go down inside that apartment," said Ryan.

"I know what we all think we saw, but let's get to the safe house and we can debrief there," replied Tom.

The team plus Chang and Chen arrived back at the safe house approximately twenty minutes later. "Did you get Dr. Shun?" asked Chang.

"We got him," said Tom. "He's a little dazed and confused right now, but alive."

Chang walked over to Shun. "I thought maybe you just didn't want to have dinner with me, Doc," he laughed.

Dr. Shun answered, "To be honest, Chang, I really wasn't hungry."

* * *

Chang was diligently working with Chen to secure transportation for the team back to Shanghai, where they would meet up with the USS Georgia in less than twelve hours. The team finished unloading the van and escorted Dr. Shun over to a couch to let him recover and get his bearings.

"What the hell happened back there?" Bill shouted. "Did you all not see what I saw when we entered the apartment?"

"I'm not sure I believe what I saw, Bill," replied Brent.

Finally, Tom spoke up. "Okay, guys, we all know what we saw, so let's just get it out on the table. We all saw Commander Maxwell and Master Chief Mitchell stepping into that ball of light."

The team all nodded their heads in agreement. But how was that possible? Clint and Paul were both running the command center back on the Georgia.

"Chief Norton," ordered Tom, "set up a comms link so we can debrief what just happened and provide an update of our current status."

"I'm on it, LT. Give me a couple of minutes."

"Georgia, this is Sitting Bull. Stand by for sitrep. Over."

"Sitting Bull, this is Georgia. Standing by. Go ahead."

"Georgia, this is Sitting Bull. Sitrep as follows: extraction mission successful; no casualties or injuries. Dr. Shun in our custody. Preparing to depart for rendezvous point, ETA ten hours from now. Will establish comms once we are safely aboard the railcar, heading to Shanghai. LT would like a word, sir. Over."

"Understand all," replied Clint. "Great job, team.

Well done. Next comms, check on railcar heading to Shanghai. Put him on."

"Georgia, this is Sitting Bull Actual. Over," replied Tom.

"Sitting Bull, this is Georgia. Go ahead, Actual."

"Sir, on another note, neither you nor the master chief will believe what we're about to tell you, but here goes. We all witnessed you and Master Chief Mitchell in Dr. Shun's apartment with us tonight. There was a big ball of light, flashbang grenades, and then you two stepped out of the ball of light. We all witnessed it, sir."

Both Clint and Paul were taken aback by what they were just told. "Gentlemen," he replied, "I'm not sure what you think you saw, but I assure you that Master Chief and I have been on the Georgia this whole time."

"Commander, I know the facts, but we all saw it with our own eyes."

There was a moment of silence, then Clint responded, "We can discuss this more once you all are safely back on board. My understanding is Chang has arranged a ride to Shanghai via the rails again. Once you all are safely en route, report your status and ETA. We'll start working our way to the rendezvous point for extraction. Georgia out."

CHAPTER 10

Dr. Shun's Disappearance

Captain Wong woke up on the floor of Dr. Shun's apartment after being unconscious for a couple of hours. He slowly sat up to focus on where he was and what he was supposed to be doing. Still dazed, he looked around and saw his men waking up as well. "Sergeant! What the hell just happened?"

"Sir, I have no idea. We entered the apartment, there was a bright light and a flash, and that's all I remember, sir."

"Is everyone all right?" shouted Wong. He stood up and looked around the room to assess the situation, then searched for Dr. Shun, realizing he was missing. "Dammit!" he shouted. "Where is Doctor Shun?"

"Sir, he was sitting on the couch reading when we entered the apartment, but that is all we remember." Neither Captain Wong nor his men had any memory of what occurred after the bright light appeared in the center of the apartment.

"Sergeant! Get your team outside and find Doctor Shun. He could not have gone far!"

"Yes, sir."

Captain Wong opened his cell phone and called Dr. Lee to provide him with an update.

"What do you mean he has eluded you, Captain?" Lee yelled when hearing about the disappearance of Dr. Shun. "You had one job, and that was to arrest him and bring him back here. If you do not find him, your career as an army officer is over. Do I make myself clear?!"

"Perfectly clear, Dr. Lee." Wong hung up, then quickly called the police chief in Wuhan. "Chief, Captain Wong here. I require your assistance and all the manpower you can provide me within the hour. I am on my way to your office now."

* * *

Meanwhile, back at the safe house, the SEAL team was getting ready to leave when Chang's cell phone rang. "This is Chang."

"This is Chen. The soldiers are awake and frantically looking for Doctor Shun. Also, Captain Wong has notified the police and requested their help because two police cars also just arrived."

"Thanks for the update, Chen; you know what to do now."

"Lieutenant!" Chang yelled. "Our military boys are awake and searching for Dr. Shun with the help of Wuhan police. We need to get to the railyard quickly, before all forms of transportation are secured and we can't leave town."

"Understood, Chang. Everyone, jump in the truck and ensure Dr. Shun is secure for the ride." The team hopped in the truck along with Chang and Dr. Shun for the ride to the railyard.

* * *

Captain Wong and his men arrived at the Wuhan police station and set up a command center to help coordinate the search for Dr. Shun.

"Sergeant, call back to base and have the proper command and control center equipment mobilized and sent over here, ASAP!"

"I'm on it, sir."

Captain Wong pulled out a photograph of Dr. Shun and handed it to the chief. "This is a picture of Doctor Shun. He is a fugitive from justice and on the loose in your city. Put out an APB for his arrest. Consider Doctor Shun armed and dangerous. Do you understand, Chief?"

"Yes, Captain, I understand."

Chen intercepted the APB via his associates and started sending out misinformation about sightings of Dr. Shun to the local police. This kept them busy for a few hours as they chased down all the leads.

* * *

Meanwhile, the SEAL team arrived safely at the railyard.

"Lieutenant, this is the railcar Chen has set up for us to ride down to Shanghai," Chang said as he jumped in. "Have your team get comfortable. I will be joining you."

"We can always use an extra pair of hands."

"Chief Norton!" shouted Tom. "Get on the SATCOM and provide Command our sitrep. Team onboard railcar, heading to Shanghai with Doctor Shun and Chang!"

"Got it." Brent established comms with Georgia and let them know the latest.

Clint and Paul had an uneasy rest for the next several hours while the train made its way to Shanghai. There was nothing more they could do until the next comms check.

* * *

Back at the police command center in Wuhan, Captain Wong was getting impatient with the police chief as all the leads coming in ended up going nowhere. "There must be more to this than meets the eye," Wong said to himself.

Eventually, Wong realized they had been had. "Attention, everyone!" he shouted. "We have been outfoxed by the good doctor. I no longer believe he is still in Wuhan. I need a list of all transportation vehicles that can travel over two thousand kilometers—planes, buses, trucks, trains—brought to me ASAP! Notify the airport to turn all planes around, and have police stop all trucks leaving the city. The good doctor is several hours ahead of us, but we will find him!"

When Captain Wong finally received the report on all transportation vehicles leaving the city, he saw that a freight train heading to Shanghai left several hours ago. A lightbulb suddenly went off over his head. "Chief! Get a couple of helicopters and have my team and I flown to Shanghai ASAP! I will need you to connect me with the Shanghai police chief while we are en route. We need to stop that freight train before it arrives in Shanghai."

CHAPTER 11

The Great Train Escape

THE SEAL TEAM was mostly asleep, attempting to get some rest prior to the next leg of their mission. Tom woke up thinking about the final steps of the extraction and how it was all going to unfold, when Chang's head bumped the side of the railcar and he woke up too. "Nice to see you awake, Chang," Tom said.

"Sorry, LT. Must've been more exhausted than I realized."

"No worries. We all took the opportunity to get a little shut-eye. Speaking of which, hey, Senior Chief, are you awake?"

"I am now," replied Bill groggily.

"I'm going to have Chang brief us on next steps. Go ahead, Chang, let's hear the plan."

Chang sat up straight and began to speak. "We're expected to arrive at the railyard around 0300 hours. I've arranged for a truck to pick us up and take us to the dock. Once I ensure that all of you are on board, the boat will take you to the rendezvous point with Georgia."

"Sounds like a solid plan. Any possibility that we could be compromised before we get there?"

Chang smiled as he lit a cigarette. "Anytime you conduct an operation like this, there's a possibility of being compromised."

Chang's cell phone rang. "Chang, this is Chen. Captain Wong has departed the city under police escort. Not sure where he is going, but he left in a hurry. They have secured all transportation in and out of Wuhan. No one in or out; a complete lockdown. He must have a lead on something."

"Thanks, Chen," Chang replied. "Keep me updated." He hung up his phone, looked over at Bill and Tom, and said, "Looks like Captain Wong may have figured out how we escaped Wuhan."

Bill shook his head. "We're several hours out at this point. I don't think that's a concern any longer."

"Captain Wong is a very resourceful officer. If there is a way to stop us, he'll find it."

"All right," Tom said wearily, then shouted, "Okay, men! Let's start getting our gear together. We may have to move out quickly, so be ready!"

The train was twenty minutes outside of Shanghai when Chen called again. "Captain Wong has figured out that you're on the freight train. He is en route to stop the train and inspect it. I have arranged to have the train stopped before that, so you can be off loaded onto a truck to finish the trip to the dock by road instead of rails."

"Thanks, Chen! When will you be stopping the train?"

"In ten minutes. Get ready!"

"Lieutenant, Captain Wong has figured out we used the freight train to get out of Wuhan. He is en route to stop the train. Chen has arranged to have the train stopped in ten minutes, and a truck will pull up alongside the railcar to take us to the dock in Shanghai."

"Well, shitfire, Lieutenant," said Bill bitterly. "Chang is just full of good news today, isn't he?"

Lots of chuckles could be heard from the other members of the team as Tom said, "Damn, Chang, I agree with Senior Chief. But I am damn glad you have Chen in the background, getting things done for us. We couldn't have accomplished what we have so far without his help."

Chang nodded. "Chen is a good man, Lieutenant. I will let him know how much you all appreciate what he has done today."

* * *

Meanwhile, Captain Wong and his team had arrived in Shanghai. They were met at the airfield by the local police chief and escorted to a helicopter that would take them out to the freight train. "Nice to meet you, Captain; we should be stopping the freight train of interest within the next ten minutes. We will land by the train and be ready to board once they stop it. I will have a few dozen men surrounding the train," said the chief, "so no one can jump off without being noticed."

"Thank you for the support, Chief. Dr. Shun is a fugitive from justice and needs to answer for his crimes."

*　*　*

Back on the train, Bill shouted, "Okay, guys! The train's slowing down, so get ready to move out! Doctor, you will follow me. Understood?"

"Understood," replied Shun.

The freight train stopped and a two-ton box truck pulled up to the railcar, just as Chen had said it would. The team jumped into the back of the truck and it sped off, heading to the dock.

"So tell me, Chang," asked Tom, "how did Chen stop the train without drawing suspicion to our departure?"

"That one's easy. There are many farms just outside the city of Shanghai, so cattle crossings are common here. Chen arranged to have some cattle cross the track at the exact place we needed to have the train stop. This is so normal, it would never be considered unusual."

"You CIA guys have everything figured out, don't you?" said Bill.

Chang just shrugged. He texted his contact in Shanghai to confirm that the boat was ready. "ETA thirty minutes," he informed the team.

After the departure of the team was complete, the train continued toward the freight depot in Shanghai. Ten minutes prior to arrival, the train was once again stopped, this time by the police. Captain Wong's men boarded the train and searched it but found no evidence of Dr. Shun. The captain himself was talking with the engineer. "How long have you been operating trains, old man?"

"The past thirty years, sonny," the engineer replied with a bit of sarcasm. "Before your parents even thought of you!"

Captain Wong was not impressed with the engineer's response, but it was not worth the effort to do anything about it.

"Captain Wong," reported his sergeant, "we have searched the entire train. Dr. Shun is not on board."

The engineer looked puzzled. "I could have told you we have no passengers on board. Our cargo is only grain and a couple of empty box cars we are transporting back to Shanghai for maintenance."

That caught Captain Wong's attention. "Did you say 'empty cars'? Sergeant! Take your men down and inspect them now!"

"Yes, Captain, on our way."

They discovered the second car unlocked with the door partially open. Increasingly inpatient, Captain Wong looked at the police chief and said, "I thought you said your men had this train surrounded."

"Captain Wong, my men reported that they saw no one get on or off the train except for your team inspecting railcars."

Captain Wong hit his fist on the side of the engine car. "Would someone like to tell me how a doctor could ride a freight train for several hours, show no sign of being here, and then disappear off a moving train without someone noticing?"

Everyone remained quiet until the engineer's assistant said, "We had to stop the train about ten minutes before you stopped us, for a farmer crossing the tracks with his herd."

Captain Wong turned and looked at the man, then back to the engineer. "Is it normal to stop for cattle crossing the tracks?"

"Yes. I usually stop two to three times when I am operating a train into Shanghai. There is even a policy among the train company that says all engineers must stop for cattle crossings."

Captain Wong jumped off the train and ran to the helicopter, jumping in the copilot's seat and shouting, "Take off, now! Head west down the track about ten miles. We will refocus our search there. He must have gotten off the train when it stopped for the cattle crossing."

The pilot acknowledged Captain Wong, powered up the helicopter, took off, and headed down the track. Captain Wong radioed the police chief and said, "Chief!

Have your men start searching for Dr. Shun about ten miles back down the track towards Shanghai. Report back to me when you have found him."

The helicopter arrived down the track a few minutes later. "Circle around this area," instructed Wong. "We may be able to spot Dr. Shun traveling on foot from the air."

The pilot acknowledged him and they started circling the area, looking for Dr. Shun. A few minutes later, Captain Wong noticed some people working below them. He had the pilot land so he could talk to them.

Captain Wong got out of the helicopter and headed towards the men he had observed from the air. "Excuse me, gentlemen!" he said as he approached them. "I would like to speak to you all for just a minute, please. Were you all here working when the freight train recently stopped for a cattle crossing?"

"We see trains stopping for cattle crossings all the time. Why are you interested in this particular train?"

"We believe a fugitive from justice boarded this train in Wuhan, and we are trying to find him and take him back to the Ministry of Health. Did you see anything unusual after this train stopped?"

Another man replied, "Well, actually, yes we did. We saw a truck pull up beside one of the cars. It stayed there for maybe two or three minutes, and then it drove off."

"Did you see any men? Can you describe anyone from the truck, please?"

"I thought I saw some men getting into the truck wearing dark, military-style clothes, but it was hard to make out how many or see any faces."

"Ok. Thank you for your time."

Captain Wong's mind started racing with this new information. He thought to himself, *Dr. Shun is not that smart; he must have had help. Multiple men in dark clothes means I must be dealing with some sort of military extraction. But who would want Dr. Shun?* Then it hit him. *The Americans!* He quickly figured out that they were heading to the ocean and called the Navy base in Shanghai.

"Commander Wu, this is Captain Wong from the command bunker at Wuhan. Sir, I need your help. I am currently twenty minutes out from your dock and will meet you at the helicopter landing pad on Changxing Island shortly."

"What seems to be the emergency?"

"Sir, I will explain upon my arrival. Please have an armed patrol boat standing by for assistance."

CHAPTER 12

Narrow Escape to the Sea

THE SEAL TEAM arrived at the dock just north of Shanghai Pudong International Airport, to meet up with a boat that was to take them out to the USS Georgia. Chang jumped out of the truck first and said, "Let me contact the boat captain. You all stay put until I signal."

Chang walked up to the boat and spoke to the captain. "Are you Captain Zhen?"

The man turned and looked at Chang. "I am Zhen. Who are you?"

Chang smiled. "Good, I am Chang. Are you ready to depart with my cargo?"

"Yes, load up so we can get underway."

Chang turned back towards the truck and signaled Tom to board the boat. "Move out," ordered Tom.

"Ryan, secure the port side!" shouted Bill. "Brent,

secure the starboard side! The rest of you, head to the back of the boat!"

The team boarded the boat. "The ship is secure, Lieutenant," reported Bill.

"Very well, Senior Chief. Chang, let's get the hell out of here before we have any more surprises."

"This is as far as I go, Lieutenant. You're in good hands with Captain Zhen. He'll ensure you arrive at your rendezvous point on time. Take care of Doctor Shun for me! Godspeed!" Chang jumped off the boat as it started backing away from the pier.

With night lights running on LOW to avoid any undue attention before they exited the harbor, the boat got underway. Tom looked over at Brent and said, "Chief Norton, once the boat is two miles out from dock, notify the Georgia that we are en route to the extraction point. ETA sixty minutes."

"Aye, sir!"

A few minutes later, Captain Zhen reported, "Lieutenant, we are two miles from the dock."

"Thanks, Zhen."

"Chief, provide Georgia our sitrep."

Now all they could do was sit tight for the next hour.

* * *

As soon as Clint received word from the team, he picked up the 27MC and said, "Captain JA." A few seconds later came back the reply, "Captain."

"Joe, this is Clint; I just received word that our team is sixty minutes from the extraction point."

"That's good news. I'll head up to the control room and prepare to pick them up. You and Master Chief stay and monitor comms with the team to relay real-time info to me."

"You got it."

*   *   *

Meanwhile, back on the pier, Chang made a new call. "The SEAL team is on the boat heading out to the extraction point, Madam Director."

"Thank you, Chang," said the mysterious voice on the other end. "All went well, I presume?"

"Yes, Madam Director. Everything went smoothly, as expected. One last thing. Did you receive my report on the situation during the extraction at Doctor Shun's apartment?"

"Yes, I did, Chang. Speak of it to no one! Are we clear?"

"Yes, Madam Director." Chang hung up the phone and left the dock area.

*   *   *

Captain Wong and his men arrived on Changxing Island shortly after the SEAL team left the dock. He had arranged for a patrol boat to be waiting for them, ready to head out to sea upon their arrival.

The base commanding officer met Captain Wong at the helicopter landing pad. "Captain Wong, I am Captain Wu. It's awfully early for me to be out helping folks from the Ministry of Health. Before I turn over a boat to you, I would like to know what is going on."

Captain Wong dialed his cell phone, talked on it for a moment, then handed it to Captain Wu. "Captain Wu," the voice said, "this is Doctor Lee, director of the Ministry of Health. Let me be extremely clear. You will provide whatever assistance is required to help Captain Wong capture a fugitive of justice. Any questions?"

"No questions, Doctor Lee. I was not made aware that you are in charge of this operation."

"As long as you understand what needs to be done, Captain, nothing else needs to be said." Lee hung up the phone.

Captain Wu handed Wong back his phone. "All right, Captain, I will escort you down to the dock and allow you to use one of my patrol boats."

Captain Wong and his team boarded the boat and took off right away. After a half-hour, the radar operator picked up a contact approximately fifteen miles offshore and heading directly east. "Captain, I have an unidentified contact bearing 095 range, ten miles speed, twelve knots."

"Very well, Radar Operator. Helm come left. Steer course 095."

"Come left, steer course 095. Helm aye, sir!"

The patrol craft was closing on the unidentified vessel, on target to intercept within twenty minutes. The patrol radioman tried to raise the other vessel on the radio, but received no response.

On the transport craft, the SEAL team and Dr. Shun were getting a little nervous now that a Chinese patrol boat was bearing down on their location. Lieutenant Wise shouted, "Chief Norton, inform Georgia of our situation!"

"Georgia, this is Sitting Bull. Stand by for sitrep. Over."

"Sitting Bull, this is Georgia. Standing by. Go ahead."

"We are twenty minutes out from extraction point. Chinese patrol craft due west of our position and closing fast. Will attempt to outrun and splash at extraction point on time. Over."

"Sitting Bull, this is Georgia. Understand all. Godspeed. Georgia out."

"Lieutenant, Georgia has been informed of our situation, sir!"

"Very well, Chief. Listen up, everyone! We need to be prepared to jump at a moment's notice. Be ready!"

After the sitrep from the team was received, Clint headed up to the control room to brief the Captain. "Captain Smith, it looks like we may get to launch a torpedo. Better get your crew ready."

"Very well, Commander Maxwell. Chief of the Watch, man battle stations!"

"Man battle stations. Aye, sir." The chief of the watch activated the general alarm.

"Officer of the Deck, the captain has the conn."

"Captain has the conn," replied the helm and the officer of the deck.

Captain Smith manned number two periscope from the officer of the deck and started conducting a visual search for the transport vessel and the patrol craft. "I have a contact bearing 300, range ten thousand yards; looks like the transport vessel described in the intel message."

"Conn Sonar, we have a new contact, bearing 290, range twenty-five thousand yards, identified as a Houjian class missile boat."

"Very well, Sonar. I think I see it now. Officer of the Deck continue to provide me with a firing solution on the patrol craft. We will designate him Master 1. Chief of the Boat, prepare to launch the SDV (SEAL Delivery Vehicle)."

"Prepare to launch the SDV. Aye, Captain."

*   *   *

On the patrol boat, Captain Wong was sitting on the bridge in a chair next to Captain Ru, thinking to himself, *I have finally cornered Dr. Shun and his unknown escorts in the Yellow Sea. What could a small trawler do against a Chinese patrol boat anyway?* The patrol boat continued to close on the SEAL team and Dr. Shun.

* * *

On the transport vessel, "Lieutenant, the patrol craft is five miles out and closing fast!" The team knew it would be close, getting off the boat onto the SDV and back to the submarine before the patrol boat could engage them.

"Chief Norton, contact the Georgia and advise them to launch the SDV now! We'll have to be prepared to abandon ship a little sooner than we thought if we can't maintain a little distance from this patrol boat."

Brent was already discussing the extraction with the master chief when the order was given. "Lieutenant! Georgia has launched the SDV. We need to close another five thousand yards before we enter the water."

Tom said, "Captain Zhen, would you be able to go a little faster and open a little range on the patrol craft before we enter the water?"

Captain Zhen looked at him, smiled, and opened the throttle of the boat. "I was waiting for you to ask." The initial thrust almost knocked the team off their feet. The boat sped up from 15 to 30 knots. "How's that for putting my foot on it, Lieutenant?"

"That'll do, Captain Zhen. That'll do."

* * *

The radar operator on the patrol craft called out, "Target vessel increasing speed. I hold the contact now at 30 knots."

"Dammit!" shouted Captain Wong. "They are attempting to outrun us! Captain Ru! Increase your speed to all ahead Flank!" The captain increased his speed to 35 knots.

"Conn Sonar," reported the sonar supervisor, "we hold Master 1 increasing speed. Looks like he has settled in at turns for 35 kts."

"Sonar Conn, aye. Officer of the Deck, update your fire-control solution for Master 1 speed 35 knots."

"Aye, sir. Updating fire-control solution for Master 1 to 35 knots."

"The transport vessel is about five hundred yards from extract point," said Captain Smith.

*   *   *

On the transport vessel, the captain motioned for Tom to come talk to him. "Lieutenant, I currently hold us five hundred yards from the drop-off point. Prepare your team to jump overboard."

"Thanks for the update, Captain Zhen."

"Looks like this'll be a close one, so here's what I intend to do. I will slow down at the drop-off point and turn to port, which will allow you and your team to jump from the starboard side undetected while I deal with the patrol boat."

"I'll have my team ready, sir. How are you going to deal with the patrol boat?"

Captain Zhen smiled. "Let me worry about that."

*   *   *

"Conn Sonar," said the sonar supervisor, "the transport vessel is slowing down and appears to be turning."

"Sonar Conn, aye," said Captain Smith. "I have visual contact on the transport vessel. I can confirm the vessel appears to be slowing and turning to port."

"Jump now!" ordered Captain Zhen. The team executed the jump; all members entered the water without detection from the patrol craft.

"Conn Sonar, I hear what appear to be splashes coming from the transport vessel. I believe the team has entered the water."

"Confirmed, Sonar. The vessel has slowed and turned around and is headed directly at the patrol craft. I cannot determine if we have men in the water."

*   *   *

Back on the patrol boat, the radar operator said, "The target vessel has slowed and changed course. I hold the contact heading on course 270, speed 20 knots. That's on a collision course with us, Captain!"

The captain of the patrol craft raised his binoculars and confirmed that the target vessel had turned around and was heading directly at them. "Man battle stations," said Captain Ru. "Radio, make one more attempt to hail the target vessel. Tell him to come to all stop and prepare to be boarded port to port, or they will be fired upon."

"Yes, sir," said the radio operator. "Unidentified vessel bearing down on Chinese patrol boat; shut down your engines and prepare to be boarded! I say again, unidentified vessel bearing down on Chinese patrol boat, shut down your engines and prepare to be boarded." There was a pause, and then he continued, "Captain, I have attempted to engage the target vessel on the radio with no success, sir."

"Very well, Radio. Weapons, prepare to fire on the target vessel on my order."

"Prepare to fire on the target vessel on your order. Aye, Captain."

"Captain Wong, it appears you will have to collect your fugitive's dead body here shortly."

The range of the transport vessel from the patrol craft was now at four thousand yards and closing fast. While the transport vessel was engaging the patrol craft in a game of chicken, the SDV pulled up alongside the SEAL team in the water, loaded them on board, turned around, and headed back to the Georgia.

On the patrol boat, the crew was preparing to fire on the target vessel. "Range to target vessel now two thousand yards and closing, Captain," said the radar operator.

"Weapons, fire the main gun turret on the transport vessel."

The patrol boat fired its main gun turret and made a direct hit on the bridge of the target vessel. The target vessel exploded and coasted to a stop while the boat was engulfed in flames.

"Chief! Man the rescue boats and take an armed escort to contain any personnel that may have survived."

"Aye, sir, on my way."

Three rescue boats entered the water and headed over to the damaged target vessel. As the rescue boats started circling the vessel for survivors, the vessel sank. The rescue boats from the patrol craft continued station-keeping for about thirty minutes, to ensure there were no survivors.

"Well, Captain Wong, I guess your fugitive got what was coming to him," said Captain Ru.

Captain Wong nodded his head in agreement and went to the radio room to call Dr. Lee. "Doctor Lee, Captain Wong here. Just wanted to update you on the situation with Doctor Shun, sir. We were unable to board the vessel our intelligence told us he was on. Instead, we were forced to destroy it. We sent over armed rescue boats to check for survivors, but found no one."

"Are you absolutely certain Doctor Shun was on that boat?"

"We have credible reports of Doctor Shun and other armed parties boarding the vessel and departing from Hangzhou Bay, north of the Shanghai Pudong International Airport."

"I hope you're right, Captain, because if Doctor Shun escaped and can tell the world about what happened here, our government will face serious consequences, and you and I will be an embarrassment to the government. Do you understand what I am telling you, Captain?"

"Yes I do, Doctor Lee."

Captain Wong walked out of the radio room and said, "Captain Ru! You may return to base. Thank you for your assistance in this matter."

"No problem at all, Captain Wong. Officer of the Deck, take us back to port," ordered Captain Ru.

* * *

Meanwhile, from the periscope of the Georgia, Captain Smith had observed and recorded the whole encounter

"Conn Sonar, sir, we are detecting the SDV approaching the sub from the port side now."

"Very well, Sonar," said the captain. "Commander Maxwell, I suggest you go greet your team and Doctor Shun by the lockout chamber."

"Thank you, Captain. Master Chief and I are on our way."

The SDV entered the DDS (Dry Dock Shelter) and was secured. The outer hatch was shut and locked, then the DDS was drained to the bilge. Once complete, the lower hatch was opened and the team, along with the SDV driver and Dr. Shun, was brought into the sub.

"Welcome back, guys," said Clint.

"Glad to be back, Skipper," replied Tom.

"Okay, you bunch of derelicts. Go get cleaned up and get something to eat. We'll debrief in one hour in the missile control center."

The USS Georgia turned towards Yokosuka, Japan, all ahead full.

CHAPTER 13

The Cruise to Yokosuka

AN HOUR LATER, the team assembled in the MCC to conduct their debriefing. "Okay, let's get started," Tom said. "Did we meet our objective to extract Dr. Shun?"

"Yes, sir, we did," replied the team.

Tom stood there for a few seconds before he spoke again. "Now, let's address the elephant in the room. Who all besides me saw Master Chief Mitchell and Commander Maxwell in Doctor Shun's apartment with their own two eyes?" Every member of the team nodded their heads in agreement.

"Guys," Clint said, "Master Chief and I were both here on the Georgia, managing the operation from here. I'm not sure what you saw, but it definitely wasn't us."

Bill stood up and cleared his throat. "Skipper, I've been supporting this team for the past three years, and I can tell you one thing for certain: the two people I saw step through that ball of light in the apartment were definitely you and the master chief."

Clint sighed. "Okay, you guys have never lied to me before. I'm not sure what you saw, but *something* unusual has occurred here which we do not understand. Master Chief, let's ensure we get statements from the entire team on what they saw so we can debrief the admiral when we get to Yokosuka."

"Will do, Skipper."

In the wardroom of the Georgia, Dr. Shun was sitting at the table with dry clothes on, sipping a cup of coffee with Captain Smith and the weapons officer, Lieutenant Chad Williams. After several moments of silence, Dr. Shun said in a firm but frightened voice, "Who are you, and where are you taking me?"

"My name is Captain Joe Smith. I'm the commanding officer of this ship. Don't worry, Doctor, you're safe here with us. You're onboard the USS Georgia submarine, and we're here to escort you to Yokosuka, Japan, for your flight back to the United States."

Shun exhaled an audible sigh of relief, knowing that he was no longer in China and didn't have to worry about Dr. Lee and the Ministry of Health trying to silence him.

Just then, the wardroom door opened and in walked Commander Maxwell and Lieutenant Wise. "Good morning, Captain. Do you mind if the lieutenant and I have a few words with Doctor Shun in private?"

"Not at all, Commander Maxwell. I have a couple of things to attend to anyway. Please stop by my stateroom when you're finished here."

"Will do." Clint and Tom both stepped over and grabbed a cup of coffee.

Dr. Shun stared at Clint with his mouth partially open and said, "You are one of the men who came out of the ball of light."

Now Clint's mouth was partially open. He was in complete disbelief; not only had his team all sworn on their reputations that they had seen him in the apartment, but now Dr. Shun said the same thing. "Doctor, as I told my men, I was here on the submarine the entire time."

Dr. Shun took another sip of coffee and looked carefully at Clint. When he spoke again, his voice had more confidence. "You are one of the men who came out of the ball of light in my apartment."

Tom said, "You see, Skipper? We're not crazy."

Clint knew something strange had happened in Dr. Shun's apartment that evening, but couldn't put his finger on it. He stood up and used the 27MC communication circuit to call Master Chief Mitchell to the room.

A minute or so later there was a double tap on the wardroom door. "Permission to enter?" said Paul.

"Enter."

Paul walked over to fix himself a cup of coffee and sat down beside Clint across from Dr. Shun at the table.

Shun looked at him and said, "You are the other person I saw step back into the ball of light in my apartment."

Paul was so shocked hearing this, he choked on a sip of coffee. "Doctor, you must be mistaken. I have been on board this submarine along with Commander Maxwell this whole time."

Dr. Shun smiled. "I am a scientist. I only state the facts, and even if I do not yet understand what happened in my apartment, I can assure you I am telling the truth and stating what I saw with my own eyes."

Clint said, "Tell us what you can remember."

Dr. Shun began recalling his story, but was interrupted by Tom when he got to the part about Captain Wong. "Why was a military officer there to apprehend you, and not the police?"

"Captain Wong was part of the original security detail assigned to escort the infected prisoners back to the prison complex a few months ago. He is on a short leash with Doctor Lee, who is the director of the Ministry of Health. Just as Wong was telling his men to arrest me, a very bright ball of light appeared in the center of my living room."

"Sir, that's the moment Petty Officer Jones and Chief Ryan also said they saw it."

"At that moment, out of the ball, appeared a couple of grenades."

"That must've been the explosion we heard through the door!"

"Lieutenant, please!" replied Clint. "Please continue, Doctor."

"I threw myself face-down on the couch and waited for the explosion. I looked up and remember seeing a flash, and then I felt lightheaded and dizzy. I tried to sit up and see what was going on. What I saw next was a man scurrying about, checking on the men who were knocked out from the blast. It was you, Master Chief. The next thing I heard was someone yell, 'All secure,' while standing next to the ball of light. That was again you, Master Chief. Another man came over and said, 'This is the doctor. He appears okay. Hurry up and return to the portal before the team arrives!' That was you, Commander."

Everyone in the room was trying to process what Dr. Shun was telling them. Clint and Paul were still in total amazement, and Lt. Wise was feeling one hundred percent vindicated.

Dr. Shun continued, "At that point, the door was forcefully opened and your team entered the room. Commander, you and the master chief turned and jumped into the ball of light, then the ball of light disappeared. That is when I saw your men. I believe it was Senior Chief Barnes who grabbed me and took me out of my apartment."

Clint took a long sip of his coffee. "Are you absolutely certain we were the two men you saw in your apartment?" Dr. Shun nodded, and Clint and Paul gave each other a look. Clint said to him, "We need to figure out what the hell happened there."

*   *   *

Captain Smith was in his stateroom reviewing reports when Clint knocked on the door. "Captain, you have a minute?"

"Come on in, Commander. Sit down."

"Joe, you won't believe the story my men are telling me regarding our after-action report, but Doctor Shun has just told us the exact same story."

"Well, let's hear it! You and I have done a strange mission or two together, so nothing coming from you will surprise me much."

Over the next several minutes, Clint explained what his team and Dr. Shun said they saw in the doctor's apartment. Joe sat listening quietly in amazement, then finally said, "I can hardly fathom what you're telling me, Clint. You expect me to believe that you and Paul somehow appeared in Doctor Shun's apartment through a ball of light, took out the Chinese military escort, ensured Dr. Shun was okay, then proceeded back into a ball of light?"

"That's what they all say happened. I can't fathom it either, but we interviewed them separately and everyone has the same story. It's like it was planted in their minds— every detail, every word."

"So how are you going to explain this in your report to the admiral?"

"I guess I'll have to do a good job keeping it classified high enough, so I only have to explain it to a handful of folks before they think I'm off my rocker."

"Good luck with that," said Joe, laughing.

"Okay, let me go discuss this with the master chief and see how we'll write it up. Have a good night. See you tomorrow."

Clint got up and headed back down to the MCC. Paul was the only one remaining when he arrived. "Well, Skipper," Paul asked, "what did Captain Smith think of your story?"

"He thinks the same thing we do. Something happened that none of us can explain. And the worst part of it is that we have to write it up and brief the admiral."

"Well, we better just tell the truth and take our lickings as they come."

"Don't worry, we'll figure this out. Get some sleep. We can talk more tomorrow."

Both Clint and Paul left the MCC and headed off to get some rest.

*   *   *

It had been three long days since Clint talked to Captain Joe Smith about what his team and Dr. Shun had seen.

The report was written, and he was ready to brief Admiral Hawkins upon arrival at 7th Fleet headquarters in Yokosuka, Japan. Joe entered the wardroom, grabbed a cup of coffee, and sat down. "Morning, Clint. We will be stationing the maneuvering watch soon. We should be pulling up to the pier in Yokosuka in about an hour. Once again, it was a pleasure to have you and your team on board."

"Thanks, Joe. I'm nervous about debriefing Admiral Hawkins this time. Usually I just give the report with my recommendations and leave. This time I'm in a position I've never been in before. I truly don't know what happened out there to my men or Doctor Shun."

"Just tell it like it is. Sometimes, believe it or not, we don't know everything. What matters is Dr. Shun is safe in custody. Your mission was accomplished."

"I suppose you're right."

Over the loudspeaker they heard, "Station the maneuvering watch!"

Joe stood up. "That's my cue to head to the bridge, Clint. I'll meet up with you after your debrief."

"Okay, Joe. See you after I get my ass handed to me," chuckled Clint.

Joe proceeded to the bridge and navigated the sub into port.

CHAPTER 14

Debrief at 7th Fleet Headquarters

A FTER THEIR EXTRACTION from China, Clint and his team arrived at 7th Fleet HQ to meet with Admiral Hawkins, Director of Naval Intelligence out of Washington, DC. Hawkins had flown over to personally thank Clint and his team.

Clint and Paul entered the formal briefing room inside the Sensitive Compartment Information Facility. Already sitting at one end of the table inside the windowless room was Hawkins—a tall, slender man in his mid-fifties, sporting thinning hair but in excellent physical shape.

"Commander, Master Chief, welcome back," said Admiral Hawkins, standing.

"Glad to be back."

"Where's Doctor Shun?"

"He's still onboard the Georgia, awaiting the security detail to transfer him to the airport."

"Very well then, Commander. Would you and the Master Chief like a cup of coffee before we get started?"

"A cup of joe would be awesome right about now, Admiral, thank you," replied Clint.

Clint and Paul each poured themselves a cup of coffee and sat down across the briefing table from Admiral Hawkins.

"Okay, let's get started with your after-action report."

Clint and Paul debriefed the admiral for forty-five minutes. Afterwards, Hawkins said, "Well, that's a hell of a mission you all carried out. Well done. Do you have anything else to report?"

Clint looked over at Paul. Paul shook his head no, but Clint said, "Well, yes sir. There is one more thing we need to tell you about." Clint and Paul told the admiral what the team had witnessed in Dr. Shun's living room, to the increasing consternation of the admiral.

"Are you two serious?"

"Yes sir, we are."

Hawkins leaned back in his chair. "Commander, for the time being I don't want either of you to repeat this story outside of this room. Is that clear?"

"Yes sir, perfectly clear."

"How many other people know this information?"

"Captain Smith and my team are all that I'm aware of, sir."

"Commander, get your team back to Langley and

report to the CIA director ASAP. I've already arranged a special flight for your team."

"But Admiral," said Paul, "we need to try to figure out what happened out there."

"In due time, Master Chief. In due time."

Clint and Paul stood up, exited the conference room, and headed back to the Georgia.

Admiral Hawkins picked up the phone and made a quick secure call. "Madam Director, I have Commander Maxwell and his team escorting Doctor Shun to your office. They should be arriving within the next twenty-four hours."

"Thank you, Admiral."

*   *   *

Clint and Paul met their team onboard the Georgia in the MCC. "Guys, listen up! The skipper has something to say."

"Okay, we're being flown back to Langley, where we will be hand-delivering Doctor Shun to the CIA director."

"Skipper, we've never briefed the CIA director personally," replied Bill. "What gives, sir?"

"Glad you brought that up. Not sure what to make of it. After Master Chief and I told the admiral what you all saw in Doctor Shun's apartment, he immediately informed us not to discuss it further. I'm not sure what's going on here, but I would suggest that you all keep your mouths shut and do not discuss this with anyone. Understood?"

Silence for the first time clouded the room. Everyone nodded in agreement. "Yes, sir."

Clint and his team were on their way to Langley.

CHAPTER 15

The Discovery

A FEW MONTHS EARLIER, back at Area 51, Dr. Rubin was sitting in his office, still in deep thought hours after the event happened, still pondering what he had seen. He got up and poured himself a cup of coffee, then sat back down in his chair and took a long sip while several hypotheses ran through his head. *Did we see into another dimension of time and space? Or was it just a complete failure of the equipment?* He continued pondering until late into the evening.

Meanwhile, Grace headed back to her office, inserted the flash drive with all the data into the Summit Supercomputer, and started running an analysis. Even she wasn't sure what she had seen in the lab a few hours ago, but she was certain she could comb through the data and find some answers.

After hours of crunching information, she still couldn't believe what she was seeing. She ran out of her office with the report towards Dr. Rubin's office.

"Doc! Doc!" Grace shouted as she ran in. "You're not going to believe what I found! You know that physicists routinely consider our world to be embedded in a four-dimensional space-time continuum, and all events that happen to us can be described in terms of their location in space-time."

"Of course, that's basic quantum physics theory. Why are you giving me a physics 101 lesson?"

Grace stood there in silence, took a deep breath, and said, "Doctor Odenwald has stated that space-time does not evolve; it exists."

"Yes, yes. What's your point?"

Grace paused for a second and continued, "What the Summit analysis is indicating is that there's actually a spaghetti-like bendable line that stretches from the past to the future, showing the spatial location of the particle at every instant in time."

"Hold on, Grace. That would mean that such a line could be sliced here and there, so you can see where the particle is in space at any particular instant."

"Yes, Doc, exactly! Once you determine the complete world line of a particle from the forces acting upon it, you've essentially 'solved' its complete history. This world line doesn't change over time but exists as a timeless object. Similarly, relativity's shape, when you solve equations for the shape of space-time, does not change in time either, but also exists as a completely timeless object. You can slice it here and there to examine what the geometry of space looks like at any particular instant."

Hans smiled and started dancing around the lab. "Grace, what this means is we can pick any point in time and examine it, past or future!"

Grace grabbed Dr. Rubin and said, "We can also look at other dimensional effects of past or future and calculate what each different dimension or other reality could look like. Doc, we've stumbled on a way to go back into the past or forward into the future and observe what could've evolved if a different set of variables were in place for the four-dimensional space-time continuum!"

"You mean to tell me we've unlocked how to look into the past and future of our world line and dial up different variables, to see what outcomes might result?"

"That's what I just said, Doc! Were you not listening to me?"

Hans sat there, staring at Grace in utter amazement. Then he stood up, walked around his desk, looked Grace in the eye, and said, "Grace, do you think you can build an algorithm that could calculate the time on the world line, and equate it to a time we could visit and explore to interact?"

"It would take some time, but I think I can come up with a prototype. I'll get started right away. Call me if you need me, Doc."

Dr. Rubin gathered his notes and headed over to the commanding officer's office at Area 51, General Timothy

Cornwall. Cornwall was a thirty-year veteran of the Air Force, highly decorated for the actions he took while flying combat missions during the global war on terror. He was being considered to replace the current top general of the Air Force upon his retirement. A tall man with blueish eyes and gray hair, Cornwall was sitting at his desk with his second cup of coffee that morning when Hans knocked on his door. "Good morning, sir. If you have a moment, I'd like to have a word with you."

"Come on in, Doctor. Would you like a cup of coffee? I just made a fresh pot."

"I'd love a cup. Thank you, General."

"Well Doctor, what's on your mind?"

"Well, General, Doctor Maxwell and I were working in the lab yesterday afternoon on the Hadron Collider. During one of our tests, something unexpected happened. Instead of seeing light at two distinct points of time, we saw what appeared to be a tear in the space-time continuum, generated by the Hadron Collider!"

"Holy cow!"

"We shut it down and Grace did a complete system check to see if we had damaged our equipment. Everything appears to be fine."

General Cornwall leaned back in his chair. "Thank God no one was hurt."

"Grace downloaded the data from the Hadron Collider and ran the analytics on the Summit mainframe here on the base. These are the results of that analysis."

He handed over the report Grace had given him earlier. Cornwall took Grace's report and started reading. Several minutes later, he sat up straight in his chair and looked at Dr. Rubin. "Doctor, if I'm reading this right, you're telling me that it might be possible for us to travel in time to the past and future, and examine different outcomes there based on different decisions, to see if the correct results can be obtained?"

"Yes sir, that's exactly what I'm saying."

General Cornwall sat thinking for a moment, then yelled out his doorway. "Susan! Cancel my budget meeting and clear my calendar. Doctor Rubin and I will be spending the rest of the day together."

"Excuse me, sir, but I don't have time to sit in your office. I need to get back to the lab and work with Grace to help her develop a prototype to test our theory."

"Oh, don't worry, Doctor, we're not staying here. I'm coming with you to your lab."

"Yes sir, General. Then I'll see you in the lab in an hour or so." Hans got up and left.

Cornwall leaned back in his chair and pondered the economic, geopolitical, and military implications of Dr. Rubin's potential discovery. That kind of power in the hands of the wrong people would be disastrous. *And who determines who the right or wrong people are?*

The general picked up his secure line and contacted the secretary of defense. "Hello, Barbra? This is General Cornwall at Area 51. Get me the secretary."

"Well, good morning, General. I'm fine, thanks for asking. Sorry, but the secretary is busy at the moment. Would you like to try back later?"

He sighed. "I'm sorry, Barbra. Good morning. How are you today?"

"Now that's better, General. I'm just fine. Thank you. The secretary will be with you shortly."

After a moment, William (Bill) Murphy, the Secretary of Defense, came on the line. "Good morning, General. What a surprise to receive a phone call from Area 51 this early in the morning. What can I help you with?"

"Sir," Cornwall began, "I know you're used to hearing strange things out of our division, but you're not going to believe what I have for you today."

CHAPTER 16

The President is Briefed

THE SECRETARY OF defense pulled into the White House garage for his scheduled meeting with the president. The secretary was thinking about how different today's briefing was going to be.

The president was in his early seventies, energetic for a man his age. "Good morning, Mr. President!" the secretary said when entering the Oval Office. "I hope you're doing well today."

"I'm doing well. So, what do you have on the agenda for today's meeting Bill?"

"Mr. President, I threw out our normal agenda to make room just for this. You're going to find it hard to believe at first, sir, but I hope you'll stick with me and hear this out."

"Oh no. Were we attacked or something?"

"No, Mr. President, nothing like that. But what I'm about to tell you will surely blow your mind."

Bill sat down across from the president's desk and

told what he knew about Dr. Rubin's discovery at Area 51.

"Nancy, arrange a video conference call with Area 51 ASAP. And cancel all calls for the next couple of hours."

"Right away, Mr. President."

Both the president and Bill proceeded out of the Oval Office.

*   *   *

Back at Area 51, General Cornwall was sitting at the head of the conference table, coffee in hand. Hans and Grace were sitting opposite each other on either side of the general—coffee for Hans and water for Grace—patiently waiting for the call to begin.

Grace was first to break the silence. "I've never had a video call with the president, or anybody, really. I spend my life in the lab. Not exactly a people-person. What are they going to ask us?"

The general looked at Grace. "I gave the secretary of defense a brief rundown on what you and Doctor Rubin discovered yesterday. He briefed POTUS this morning and he wants to know more about your discovery."

"There's not much more to tell, at least not right now. I haven't had a chance yet to develop an algorithm to test if we can replicate the results. I'm not positive we can even do it again. It's going to require a lot more time and work. I wish you hadn't told anyone until we had a chance to gather more facts and test our theory first."

The general looked at Grace with a puzzled look. He was not used to anyone telling him he might have let the cat out of the bag too soon. "Well, Grace, I believe that you and Doctor Rubin will replicate and control your discovery in due time. The best way to secure continued support for your research is to keep the highest powers in the loop on your progress. Therefore, I briefed the Secretary."

Grace sat back in her chair and rolled her eyes, ensuring that everyone in the room noticed her displeasure about the situation. Hans didn't say a word because he had known this call was coming, and there was nothing more they could disclose regarding the discovery.

The phone rang and the video projector turned on, displaying the White House situation room as the secretary and the president entered. "Good morning, everyone," said the president.

"Good morning, Mr. President."

"Mr. President, I'm General Cornwall. I am the commanding officer here at Area 51. To my right is Doctor Hans Rubin, our chief quantum physics director here at the lab. To my left is Doctor Grace Maxwell, Doctor Rubin's chief assistant."

"Well, General, the Secretary has gotten me up to speed on recent developments there. I understand it has something to do with being able to travel back in time or into the future. Is that correct?"

Dr. Rubin spoke up. "Something like that, Mr. President."

"What do you mean, Doctor?"

"The principal statement you made is correct, but what we're able to do is actually even more astounding. Not only are we able to move back and forth across the timeline, but we're able to investigate other realities that may exist or could exist. Doctor Maxwell and I are currently evaluating if we can control timeline entry points. We might be able to introduce variables to alter reality in other dimensions."

"I'm not sure what to make of that statement, Doctor. If I understand correctly, you've discovered a way to go back into any point in history and alter the truth behind the unknown, making it possible to look into the future and dial up different outcomes, exploring how they would've manifested. Am I getting that right?"

Grace answered, "Well, yes, Mr. President, that's exactly what we're suggesting. I've started working on an algorithm that would allow us to do just that."

"That's wonderful news, folks! When can we expect a demonstration?"

"I'm not exactly sure, Mr. President," replied Grace. "We just started working on it. Once we have a prototype developed and conduct some tests, we'd be thrilled to have you join us here."

"That would be great. I'm looking forward to it. In the

meantime, how many people currently know about this discovery?"

General Cornwall replied, "As far as I know, Mr. President, it would be the three of us in this room, Mr. Secretary, and yourself."

"Good. I want to keep this classified at the highest levels, and all information regarding resource requirements will be authorized by no one except the secretary of defense and myself. If no one else has anything, I need to get back to my office. I have a meeting with the Chinese prime minister in an hour. General, keep us directly in the loop on this. Again, great discovery, Area 51! Keep up the good work."

On that note, the call came to an end and the video screen went dark.

"Doctor Rubin, Doctor Maxwell," said Cornwall, "this will be your number one priority from now on. Report to me and only me with your progress, and I'll brief the secretary as needed." General Cornwall walked out, leaving Grace and Hans sitting at the conference table alone.

"Well, I guess we need to head back to the lab and get to work."

Grace looked at him and rolled her eyes as she let out a long, tired sigh. "We've got a lot to figure out."

CHAPTER 17

Langley CIA Headquarters

Back at present day, Commander Maxwell and his team, along with Dr. Shun, arrived at Langley in two SUVs shortly past 10 a.m. after their lengthy flight from Yokosuka. They entered the lobby and were greeted by two agents. "Good morning, everyone. Commander Maxwell, if you and your team would kindly follow me, the director is looking forward to meeting with you all today."

The team was escorted to a secure conference room near the CIA director's office. The sizeable room had no windows and a large wooden oval table with ten matching chairs, remarkably like the one in Admiral Hawkins's office. Clint and his team all took seats at the table along with Dr. Shun. A couple of folks came in and offered the team coffee and doughnuts. "Finally, some decent food!" shouted Paul. They all laughed and started eating.

A couple of minutes later, the door opened and a

short, older but attractive woman entered. They all stood and gave their respectful welcome to the director.

"First," she began, "let me congratulate you all on a job well done. Thank you. And Doctor Shun, welcome to the United States."

"Thank you, Madam Director."

A pair of agents walked into the room. "Doctor Shun," she continued, "you will go with these gentlemen and start debriefing our team on what the hell is going on over in Wuhan, so we can get a better handle on what to expect. So far the general public here is still largely unaware of what this is and how fast it's spreading, but the media will catch on fast enough and we need to be ready. I have a call with the CDC in two days and I want to control the first reports on this, for your sake and ours. We have kept our promise to extricate you safely, Doctor. We appreciate your cooperation now in telling us what you know."

Dr. Shun stood up and said, "Commander, thank you and your team again for rescuing me from Wuhan. I can't express my gratitude enough. I will be happy to provide whatever information you need to help with the virus outbreak."

After the doctor's departure, Clint stood and said, "Well, if that's all you need from us, Madam Director, we'll head out and return to Little Creek ASAP."

"Not so fast, gentlemen. You all have some explaining to do! I know all about the incident inside Doctor Shun's apartment that night, so why don't you explain to me exactly what's going on?"

"Madam Director, I have orders from the DNI (Director of Naval Intelligence) himself not to discuss that part of the mission with anyone."

"I see. Carol! Get Admiral Hawkins on the line and patch him into the conference room. Thank you."

Clint and his team sat in the conference room for a few minutes in complete silence, staring at the director, when the conference phone finally rang. "Well, hello, Admiral. I hope all is well over at ONI today?"

"Yes, all is well here. How can I help you today?"

"Admiral, kindly inform Commander Maxwell that he may debrief his mission with me."

The speaker went silent for about ten seconds, then finally the admiral replied, "Commander Maxwell, you are authorized to discuss with the CIA director all information relating to your mission in Wuhan."

The director hung up the phone and said, "Before we get started, I need a refill on my coffee." She pushed a button on her table and a couple of people came in with refills and more doughnuts for everyone.

As Clint relayed the story of the last 48 hours, the director sat back in her chair with her legs crossed, holding her coffee in both hands and slowly sipping it. When he was done, she placed her cup on the table, pulled herself close to them, and said, "So all of you highly trained warriors saw the same impossible thing?"

"Yes, Madam Director, that's what it boils down to."

The director took off her glasses and rubbed her eyes. "When I was first told about this, I couldn't believe it. Don't get me wrong; something happened in that apartment that night, and all of you have the same story. Either you all are covering your asses to make up for a screwup, or you are all just as puzzled as I am.

"I can see now, though, that I have no choice but to assume it's true. From here on you will not discuss this with anyone outside of this room."

The director turned towards Clint and said, "Commander, you and your team will return to Little Creek and relax for now. Job well done. Admiral Hawkins and I have authorized a thirty-day furlough for you all. Once your furlough is complete, you will report back here to my office for further orders. Remember, not a word to anyone. Any questions?"

The team was ecstatic about the thirty-days R&R, but puzzled regarding possibly working for the director of the CIA. Nonetheless, they accepted their orders and filed out.

CHAPTER 18

The Quantum Transporter is Born!

AFTER LONG MONTHS of hard work, Grace and Hans were ready to test the algorithm that would allow them to open a portal and travel back or forward in time. "Grace, do you have all of the equipment set up for our test?" asked Hans.

"Just finishing up aligning the four Hadron Collider Ion cannons for the Higgs field test."

Hans was excited. It all came down to this test. The lab was filled with four massive ion cannons and their associated equipment, all centered around a circular array. The cannons were pointed at specific points per Grace's calculations, which would reflect the rays into the center, to supply a stable Higgs field for the test.

"Okay, Doc, initiating power-up sequence now. So far so good. All systems are stable and ready for the test."

"I agree, Grace. Proceed."

"Starting sequence now!"

The ion cannons came alive, each firing at a specific point on the uniquely designed array. "Doc, we've established a stable Higgs field at ten percent power efficiency."

"Increase power at ten percent increments until we reach fifty percent."

"Increasing power to the Hadron ion cannons now. Twenty percent. Now thirty. Forty percent and still stable. Fifty percent and still stable, Doc."

"Let's proceed to seventy-five percent."

"Hold on, I'm showing one of the cannons fluctuating. Wait, that got it. Seventy-five percent power and stable."

"Okay, Grace, increase to full power and let's see if we can open up the time-space continuum."

"Increasing power to one hundred percent."

Both Hans and Grace looked at the center of the Higgs field to see if there was any change. Suddenly, in the center there appeared to be an open window seven feet by seven feet in size.

"Grace! That's it! We've opened a window of time! If my calculations are correct, we should be looking at New York City just after the announcement that Japan had surrendered at the end of World War Two."

Both Grace and Hans looked through the window at a ticker-tape parade happening in Times Square. "I can't believe it!" gasped Grace. "It worked! It worked!"

Hans sat down in the chair by the controls he was

monitoring, closed his eyes, and thanked the Lord for this wonderful discovery. "Grace," he said, "let us move on with phase two. We need to be able to select different points on the timeline, both past and future. Are you ready to commence?"

"Yes, I will now dial up our next test target in time— December 7th, 1941, at 0800 Hawaii time, to monitor the bombing of Pearl Harbor. Entering in the variables now. Stand by to jump. Three, two, one, execute!"

The quantum window jumped to Pearl Harbor like changing the channel on a TV. "Oh my God, Grace!" said Hans in an excited voice. "We're watching the bombing of Pearl Harbor like it was a movie!"

"Like an old silent movie, but in color."

"Can you achieve audio?"

"Not sure yet, Doc. Let me review all of the data once we've finished."

"Okay, Grace, next test takes us back to July 1st, 1863, at the battle of Gettysburg."

"Dialing now, Doc. We should see Gettysburg shortly."

The horrible scenes of Pearl Harbor vanished and a new projection was displayed in the window—a large open field with two opposing armies shooting it out.

"It appears our protocols are working effectively. If we could just have audio, this would be priceless."

"Dialing back now to November 11th, 1620, so we can watch the Pilgrims on the Mayflower landing in Cape Cod." The quantum window once again changed to the coast of Cape Cod.

"Remarkable, Grace. We're seeing what has only been read about in history books."

"Doc, I want to try dialing up a location during the BC era. I'll try the night Cyrus the Great entered into Babylon—October 12th, 539 BC, just after midnight."

The window now showed an ancient army marching along rock-strewn mountains. "This is unbelievable, Grace! We'll be able to go back into history, review it for accuracy, and fix records to reflect what actually happened. Let's conduct one final test. Let's look into the future and see what is happening in New York City in 2035. Times Square, Dec 31st at 2350 hours, so we can watch the ball drop."

"Dialing it up now."

There was a pause, and then Hans said, "What the hell is that? Grace, are you sure you dialed up the correct location?"

"Positive, Doc. We're looking at New York City in 2035. New Year's Eve, ten minutes before midnight."

All they could see was destroyed buildings surrounded by rubble. No celebration. No people at all. "Something clearly happens in New York City before or during 2035 that we're unaware of."

"We can look later, after we finish testing the Quantum

Variable Scenario Replicator. In the meantime, shut down the test and see if you can solve the audio problem."

Over the next couple of weeks, Grace solved the audio problem and also figured out how to enter different variables that would allow the creation of other, altered dimensions to foresee the outcome of each variable for the future. A functioning beta model of the QVSR was created.

"Grace, you've done some terrific work here. I know your father will be proud of you."

"Thanks, Doc. I was able to test the QVSR on a couple of different scenarios, and the results appear to be accurate. Now we need to put boots on the ground to confirm our theories. I've put together a plan to use wormhole theory to create an event horizon that will allow the passage of personnel, equipment, and communications into the visiting time period, and also into our altered dimension."

"Fantastic work, Grace. Is the gateway one-way?"

"No, it'll allow two-way travel as long as the gateway is open."

"It could be dangerous if something came back from our altered reality and existed here in this time-space."

"No worries. I've created a shield that, when energized, will only allow items we designate to pass through the gateway." She stood there with her arms crossed and a big grin on her face.

"Nice work indeed. We'll need to test it once we

have a team here to do it. I guess we need to let General Cornwall know we're ready to move into field tests."

The next phase of the project would transition objects and people through the barrier. The quantum transporter was born!

CHAPTER 19

The QSTCC is Created

After Drs. Grace Maxwell and Hans Rubin wrapped up the successful testing of the quantum transporter, Hans went to discuss the results with General Cornwall.

When he arrived, the general looked up and said, "Come on in, Doc. What have you got for me?"

He walked into the office and sat down in the leather chair across from the general's desk. "General, we've completed our initial phase of testing."

"That's great news! What's next on the testing agenda?"

"Actually, sir, we're ready to start LIVE exercise field testing with actual teams."

The general sat back in his chair and clasped his hands on his desk. "I didn't think you'd be this far along so soon. I'll have to update the secretary of defense before we can proceed with LIVE field tests."

"I understand. Grace and I have some more work to do, but we'll be ready to begin the next phase within the next sixty days."

"All right, Hans. I'll brief the secretary this afternoon. I have a meeting with him to discuss other matters, and this is now first on the list."

"Thank you, General. Let me know if you need anything else from Grace or me." He stood up and left, going back to the lab.

Once his office door closed behind Dr. Rubin, Cornwall picked up the secure phone and called the secretary's office.

"Secretary of Defense, this is Barbra. How may I assist you today?"

"Hello, Barbra! This is General Cornwall. How are you doing this fine day?"

"Hello, General. I am doing great. Thanks for asking. Do you need to speak with the secretary?"

"Why yes, if it isn't too much trouble."

"No trouble at all, General. Stand by," as she placed him on hold.

A couple of minutes went by before the secretary came on the line. "Hello, General! Sorry, I was on another call, with the joint chiefs. What can I help you with?"

"Mr. Secretary, the initial testing on the QVSR and the quantum transporter was successful. We will be ready to commence LIVE field exercise testing within the next sixty days."

The secretary paused before answering. "I thought the testing would take longer?"

"I said the same thing, sir, but Dr. Rubin has assured me that testing went extremely well and we can move into the next phase sooner than expected."

"Very well. I will notify the president and figure out what we are going to do next." The secretary hung up the phone and rang the White house.

"Hello, Nancy, I hope you are well today. May I speak to the president?"

"Hello, Mr. Secretary, I am, thanks for asking. One moment, sir."

"Bill! What a pleasant surprise. What can I help you with?"

"Mr. President, I just received an update from General Cornwall over at Area 51. All of the initial tests have proven successful."

"That's very good news! Are they ready to provide us with a demonstration?"

"No, sir, not yet. Doctor Rubin is requesting personnel to participate in LIVE field trials. We have approximately sixty days to assemble a team to help with the project."

"Very well, Bill. I suggest we have a meeting with Admiral Hawkins, the CIA director, and yourself to bring everyone up to speed on what we know and figure out how we are going to use this technology moving forward. Please make it clear to everyone that this project must be kept classified at the highest levels."

"I understand, sir. I will set up the meeting."

The next day, with the president's most trusted team assembled in the Oval Office, he wasted no time as he entered the room. "Good morning, all. You're here today because Doctor Rubin and Doctor Maxwell at Area 51 have developed a technology that can scan back and forth through time and transport personnel to any place in the world at any given moment."

There was a brief stunned silence before the CIA director (Janet Crawford) spoke up first. "This is the first time I'm hearing about any discovery at Area 51."

"I classified it for my eyes only until the theories could be proven and replicated. Now it's no longer theoretical. As of yesterday morning, it exists. You are both aware that Commander Maxwell's latest mission featured an unusual observation, are you not?"

Admiral Hawkins and the CIA director looked at each other, and Janet said, "Yes, Mr. President, we are aware of some sort of anomaly associated with Commander Maxwell's mission in Wuhan."

"Okay, well these events are tied together. I'm bringing you all in on this now, so we can develop an organization to operate it from a top secret, black ops perspective. It'll have the full support and resources of the US government, but I must also have plausible deniability."

POTUS looked over at the CIA director. "I know,

Janet, that you think you should be in charge of this new endeavor yourself, but your organization still has too many leaks." He looked over at Admiral Hawkins next. "You also have too many leaks." And then the president turned to address the secretary of defense. "This brings me to you, Bill. I want the new Space Force to oversee this command. They will report directly to me at the White House. No one else."

"Mr. President, do you really want General Lawless in charge of such an important project related to national security?" challenged Janet.

The president turned to face her. "Yes, I do." Then he looked around the room at each of them. "And you all have my word that I will keep you well-informed each step of the way. We'll establish a committee to provide oversight that includes all of you, but I reserve the right to make ultimate decisions after hearing your recommendations."

Each member of the team questioned the placement of the new command, but to no avail. There was no changing the president's mind.

"Well, it's settled then," he said. "Janet, who would you put in charge of this new command?"

"I would nominate Commander Clint Maxwell. He's the current Navy SEAL team commander over at Little Creek, highly decorated for his leadership and decision-making abilities. He was also the commander who oversaw the extraction of Dr. Shun from Wuhan."

"I support that choice, Mr. President," replied Admiral Hawkins.

"Okay, then Commander Maxwell will lead the new Quantum Space-Time Continuum Command, attached to the Space Force under General Henry Lawless. The QSTCC has a nice ring to it, don't you think?"

"I guess it does, sir," replied Bill.

"Okay, folks, meeting adjourned. Let's get this new command operational right away."

CHAPTER 20

The Appointment

Langley CIA Headquarters

CLINT HAD JUST returned from visiting his parents in Santa Fe, New Mexico, where his father worked at the Los Alamos Laboratory. He had been with them for the past month and now wondered why the CIA director wanted to see him as soon as he checked in. Driving over to Langley, his phone rang. "Commander Maxwell," he answered.

"Commander, Admiral Hawkins. I hope you enjoyed your R&R."

"I did, sir. I hadn't been back to Santa Fe for a while. My folks were starting to wonder if I was still alive."

"How is Dr. Maxwell? I served with your father when he developed the F-22 Raptor project. I was his test pilot, you know."

"I'm fully aware of that, sir. My father sends his regards and hopes to visit you soon."

"I just wanted to confirm you were heading over

to Langley today. The CIA director wants to see you ASAP."

"So I've been told. I'm on my way right now, sir. Approximately sixty minutes out."

"Perfect. I'll talk to you once you arrive."

The CIA director and Admiral Hawkins were waiting for Clint in a conference room when he arrived. "Well," he said, chuckling, "looks like I'm not the only military person out of place today."

The admiral laughed and nodded. "Take a seat, Commander. The director and I have some interesting news for you."

Clint poured himself a cup of coffee and took a seat at the table. "So, what is this all about? You had me drive all the way over here from Little Creek. I'm definitely curious."

Janet leaned back in her chair, looked at Clint, and said, "Commander, let me get straight to the point. You are our top pick to run a new organization that was just created by the POTUS and the secretary of defense."

"Okay. Go on, I'm listening. Something tells me this isn't going to be just another SEAL team base in a new location."

The director smiled. "No, Commander. Not quite." She got Clint up to speed on the establishment of the QSTCC.

Clint sat back and looked over at Admiral Hawkins. "I'm a SEAL Commander. What would I do in Nevada?

And I thought this Area 51 was just a testing facility. I'm not sure I get what you're trying to do or why you want me in charge."

Clint was caught off-guard with this sudden change of orders. "Admiral, with all due respect, sir, I've been with my unit a little over three years, and we've made significant progress in performance and capabilities. We operate like a well oiled machine together. I don't believe it's in anyone's best interests to pull me away from them now."

"I wouldn't worry about that, Clint," the admiral assured him. "Your unit is going with you to Area 51."

The admiral and the director gave Clint a minute to process the latest bit of news. His mind was racing for answers to questions he hadn't even begun to ask. He was confused, puzzled, and a little ticked off. After all, he and his guys were amphibious, not a pack of desert rats. Part of him was intrigued by the mystery of this new assignment, and another part of him was sounding warning bells and raising red flags. "What is it I'll be in charge of over there?"

The director handed a folder over to Clint. "Everything you need to know to get started is in this folder. I suggest you read this before you leave today, and once you're finished, I will have a member of my staff ship it to Area 51, so you'll have it in your new office upon your arrival next week. Commander, I have another meeting, but Admiral Hawkins will remain here with you to answer any questions. I understand this is unexpected and moving fast, but I trust that you are up to this task and we can expect only the best from you and your men. That's what you've proven so far. Let's keep it that way." The director stood and excused herself from the conference room.

Clint looked at Admiral Hawkins with a baffled expression. "Admiral, what exactly have you gotten me into?"

Hawkins stood up to pour another cup of coffee, then sat back down in the chair across from Clint. He leaned back while taking a sip and said, "Do you remember when you told me about what took place in Doctor Shun's apartment that night?"

"Yes, sir. I also remember you telling me not to discuss it with anyone."

"Well, Commander, the job you're going to do will help you understand exactly what happened in that apartment. I want you to read the material in this envelope while I arrange to have lunch brought in for us. Are you okay with a turkey sandwich from Jason's Deli?"

"Sure, that's fine."

The admiral left the conference room to order lunch. Clint thought to himself, *What does Doctor Shun's apartment have to do with this new assignment, and why Area 51? What possible use could I be out there?*"

Clint opened the folder and started reading. Before

he got too far into the origin of his new command and what it would be responsible for, he placed the folder on the table in front of him, rubbed his eyes, and stated out loud to no one, "You've got to be freakin kidding me!"

When the Admiral returned to confirm lunch was on the way, he found Clint staring at the wall. "So Clint, have you read the whole file? What do you think about your new command and directives?"

"If what I read in this folder is true, then it's possible that my men did see Master Chief and myself that night in Doctor Shun's apartment."

"Based on the science I've seen from Area 51, I would say that is correct, Commander."

"Admiral, do you realize what you're asking me to believe in order to move forward with this?"

Just then, the CIA Director's secretary came in with lunch. He waited for her to set the tray down before he answered Clint's question. "Look, Commander, I realize this is a lot to process, but the task is real and the science is real. You need to accept the role and responsibility you've been given. You were recommended for this unanimously by the CIA director, the secretary of defense, and me personally. Our choice was blessed by POTUS himself. Not sure what else can be said here, Clint. The entire top chain of command believes in you. Let that sink in a bit."

Hawkins stood up to leave. "I need to make a couple

of calls; I'll be back shortly. If you have any questions, feel free to ask me then."

Clint appreciated the admiral giving him a minute alone, but he didn't need to deliberate. He was committed to his service in the United States Navy and would go where he was asked to go. It was somewhat a relief that his guys would be going with him, but he wasn't sure they would feel that way. *This assignment will help us understand what happened in Doctor Shun's apartment that night. The entire National Security team believes I'm the right man to command, and the president gave his personal blessing. This is the command of a lifetime.*

By the time the admiral walked back into the room, Clint's demeanor had changed from "WTF am I doing here" to "I'm the man for this job." "Any questions for me, Commander?"

"No, sir. I'm eager to get back to Little Creek and tell my team about our new assignment."

"Commander, not a word to the team about what this project is until after their arrival at Area 51. This remains highly classified on a strictly need-to-know basis."

"Understood, sir."

"Clint, we're positive we made the right choice for the first commanding officer of the QSTCC. We have complete faith and trust that you and your team will make us proud."

"I'll do my best not to let you all down, Admiral."

"I'm sure you won't. Remember, you'll be on General Cornwall's base, but you report to General Lawless, the head of the Space Force. Is that going to be any problem?"

"No, sir. Understood." Clint slid the folder back over to Hawkins across the table, to ensure it was delivered to Area 51. Then he turned and exited the conference room.

Janet returned a few moments later. "Admiral, did Commander Maxwell leave already?"

"Yes."

"How did he react to our wonderful news?"

The admiral smiled. "He appeared to be slightly stunned at first, but soon realized he has to be a part of it."

Janet smiled, grabbed the folder from the admiral, and left the conference room.

* * *

Clint arrived back in his office just before 1600 and requested Master Chief Mitchell report to see him ASAP. When Paul arrived, he stood in the doorway but Clint didn't notice him, so he cleared his throat. "You wanted to see me, Skipper?"

"Yes, Master Chief. Sorry, I was still thinking about the conversation I had with Admiral Hawkins this morning."

"You look a little uneasy. Is something wrong?"

Clint took in a deep breath and let it out. "Sorry, I had a lot of information thrown at me today."

"No worries. You know I understand. Break it down for me and maybe I can help. That's my job."

Clint smiled and leaned back in his chair. "I've always known I can talk to you, Paul, but thanks for saying it anyway."

"So, how can I help? You did request my presence in your office, didn't you?"

Clint leaned forward in his chair. "Master Chief, prepare our team to mobilize. We transfer to a new location over the weekend."

"Another mission?"

"Yes and no. We'll be setting up a brand new command with unprecedented objectives."

"Sounds interesting so far. A new SEAL team operations center?"

"Not exactly. We'll no longer be part of the SEAL team command structure once we leave this base."

Paul leaned back in his chair, looking puzzled for the first time. "But Clint, we're a SEAL team. I'm not following you."

"I've been assigned as the new commanding officer of the QSTCC."

"The QSTCC? What the hell is that? And what does it have to do with our team?"

"It stands for the Quantum Space-Time Continuum Command. I've been tasked by the president himself to stand up and operate out of Area 51 in Nevada. I'll report to General Lawless, the head of the Space Force."

Paul sat in complete amazement for a brief moment, then quickly regained his composure. "Sir, we're a SEAL team. Why would we be assigned to the Space Force at Area 51 in the middle of the desert?"

"Believe me, my initial reaction was the same as yours. But do you remember what the team told us about that bright light event in Doctor Shun's apartment?"

"Yes, of course. Hard to forget."

"Well, I can't go into details yet, but once we report to Area 51 and settle in, I'll hold a briefing with the team and explain how that bright light connects to our new assignment. This move to our new home is strictly classified, Top Secret. No one can know where we're going or why until I authorize an official cover story. All clear?"

"Yes, sir. I'll work with Senior Chief Barnes to develop plans and make sure our weapons and gear go with us."

Clint held up his hands. "No need to do that. Only personal weapons and equipment. Once we arrive at Area 51, you and Senior Chief can stock up our armory with everything we'll need."

"Aye, sir."

After Paul left his office, Clint's secure phone rang.

"Commander Maxwell, General Lawless."

"Good afternoon, General. I understand that I'll be reporting to you starting next week."

"That's correct, Commander, and don't worry, I'll ensure you and your team will be well taken care of at Area 51. I'll meet you there myself next Monday morning to show you around. It'll allow us to get to know each other."

"That sounds good, General. Also, it would be good for my team to hear straight from you what their new purpose will be, if that's okay."

"Commander, I'll be happy to address your team directly. Pleased to have all of you on board."

"Sounds like a plan then. Thank you, General. If there's nothing else, sir, I have a lot of work to do before I move to Nevada."

"I have nothing else, Commander. Welcome. I'll see you Monday."

Clint hung up, sat back in his chair, and took a long drink from his water bottle. He thought to himself, *This new adventure I'm about to embark on is going to be different from anything I've done before. Time to grab the bull by the horns and hang on.*

CHAPTER 21

Team Arrives at Area 51

As their transit plane touched down on Monday morning at the Area 51 airfield, the team was exiting the craft and Bill said, "Damn, Master Chief, I feel like I'm back in Iraq! Hot, dry, and barren. I hope the washing machines around here work."

Paul chuckled and said, "Senior Chief, you always have a way with words."

General Cornwall met the team at the airfield. "Good morning, gentlemen. My name is General Cornwall. I'm the commanding officer here at Area 51. I'm glad to have you all here."

Clint walked up to the general and saluted. "Commander Maxwell, sir, we're happy to be here."

General Cornwall escorted Clint and his team to the main admin building where his office was located, then had them assemble in the conference room. After everyone put down their equipment and settled into the chairs, Cornwall addressed the team. "Welcome again to Area 51, gentlemen. I have to confess, I know you guys operate all over, but I never expected to host a SEAL team here."

"To be honest, General, we never expected to be assigned here, but here we are," replied Clint. "Do you know what time General Lawless will arrive?"

"He should be here within the next couple of hours. In the meantime, I'm sure you all are hungry. Please, help yourselves." He pointed to a generous buffet at the back of the room.

The team turned and looked at the counter filled with scrambled eggs, bacon, ham, toast, fruit, yogurt, juice, milk and coffee—a spread fit for a king. "Thanks, General," replied Paul. "I know I'm hungry. How about you guys?"

A round of "Hell yes" was shouted as the team dug into the buffet.

During breakfast, Cornwall got the team up to speed on their new assignment, then afterward brought them down to the lab to meet Dr. Rubin and Grace, who were both eagerly awaiting them. "Good morning, General!" Hans said. "So glad you could bring us visitors this morning." He turned to Clint. "Nice to see you again, Commander Maxwell and Master Chief Mitchell."

"Hello, Clint," Grace said as they entered. "Nice to see you finally decided to come visit me at work." She wrapped her arms around Clint and gave him a warm hug and a kiss on the cheek.

"Gracey? Dad said you were working on a special project, but I had no idea it was here. I see you're putting their college investment to excellent use."

"You always had a way with introductions, big brother."

The team looked at Grace and Clint in utter disbelief. Clint had never mentioned a sister, much less a beautiful one.

As Grace pulled away from Clint's embrace, she looked around the room at her brother's team. "I feel like I know each of you already, because when I do get to visit with my brother, you're all he talks about!"

"Guys, my sister is off-limits. Is that clear?" Clint warned.

The team mumbled and nodded their heads in agreement.

"Hello, everyone, my name is Doctor Hans Rubin," interjected Hans. "I see you all have met Grace. Clint, it's nice to see you again. I think the last time we saw each other was at Gina's funeral."

"I believe you're correct, Hans. It's good to see you again as well." Dr. Rubin had been a close friend of Clint and Grace's father when they were growing up.

"So, Doc, what's all the fuss regarding why my team and I are here?"

"Grace and I will give you all an overview of what

we've discovered, and when General Lawless arrives we can move our discussion to more of a tactical nature. I know this is a little far-fetched from your usual missions, but please keep an open mind as we explain why you're all here." Hans and Grace spent the next couple of hours explaining their discovery and what it meant to the world. The team sat completely in awe over what they were hearing. After a while, Paul stood up and said, "Doctor Rubin, no offense, but come on. You expect us to believe that we can travel in time to any point in the future or past and not only observe, but potentially alter and manipulate it?"

General Lawless chose that moment to enter the room. "That's correct, Master Chief. Not only can we view it, but we are expecting to send personnel through the open portal to interact with other points and places in time."

"So, this is what we saw in Doctor Shun's apartment that night," replied Senior Chief Barnes, catching on. "But how? We haven't even been here yet."

"Remember what I said," replied Hans. "We can dial into any time component, past or future, and interact with it."

"I'm not gonna lie. This is completely freaking me out," said Senior Chief Barnes. The rest of the team concurred in unison.

Dr. Rubin interjected, "I know it's hard to believe, but Grace and I have tested this extensively since our discovery, and it's quite precise and reliable. Grace did a fantastic job writing the algorithm that allowed us to control it once the rift was open."

"Well, Commander, what do you think of our little operation here?" asked General Lawless.

"To be honest with you, General, I'm still trying to wrap my head around this whole concept," replied Clint as he looked over the equipment.

General Lawless looked at the team and smiled. "You all were chosen for this project because you're the best of the best, and I know that your team will make America proud. Obviously, this project is highly classified, so no one can discuss anything that goes on here outside of this facility. I trust you all are used to this, gentlemen?"

Everyone nodded their heads in agreement. "Yes, General. Not a word, sir!"

General Lawless pulled up a chair and sat down. "Commander, I have your first assignment in this envelope. I suggest you have your team get settled in here at the base and start preparing for departure."

"You heard the man, guys! Let's find our quarters, get settled, and prepare for our first mission," said Paul.

Paul and the rest of the team were escorted out by General Cornwall while Clint and General Lawless stayed behind in the lab with Dr. Rubin and Grace. "Here you are, Commander, your first mission." The general handed Clint the envelope.

Clint opened it, his eyes opening wide as he read it. "General, is this some kind of a joke?"

"No, Commander, it is not. I expect a report once this mission is completed. I suggest you and your team work with Doctor Rubin and Doctor Maxwell over the next several days to get familiar with the tech before you proceed. Unless you have any questions for me, I'll get out of your hair now."

"No, general. No questions."

General Lawless stood up and left. Clint's mind swirled with everything he had been told, and the realization that his baby sister was at the helm of this incredible development. Little Gracey! That was blowing his mind. On the downside, what was he getting his team into? Could they do this? Were they wrong to not stop and think about the implications? Analyzing risks was not part of his job, and as the one executing the orders, it gave him some real pause.

Clint was not a man used to doubting or hesitating. His unit counted on him to be sure and confident so they could be also. He took a long drink of water, exhaled a long sigh, stood up, and headed for his new office.

CHAPTER 22

Gearing Up to Start Operations

C LINT'S NEW OFFICE was like his other one back in Virginia, except this one had no windows—just a large, stained-oak desk with a plush leather executive chair behind it. He had a top-of-the-line computer with dual monitors and a giant whiteboard on the opposite wall where he and the team could draft plans and explore operational scenarios with potential outcomes. There was also a Bunn coffee station stocked with all the fixings by the door, the best the Space Force could provide. *Not bad*, Clint smiled to himself.

Outside his office was a smaller desk that had a computer, phone, filing cabinets, and a small whiteboard. That would be for his assistant once he selected the right candidate.

Clint texted Paul and asked him to stop in. A few minutes later, Paul knocked on the door. "You wanted to see me, Skipper?"

"Yes, Master Chief. Come on in and sit down."

Paul entered and sat in the chair across from Clint's desk. He looked around the room. "Wow, this is a mighty fine office. Your own coffeepot and everything!"

Clint laughed. "Did you and the rest of the team get settled in?"

"Yes, we did. There are some things we still need, but I provided a list to the supply officer over by General Cornwall's office."

"Good to hear. Listen, Paul, we've worked well together for years now. I trust you completely. I hope you won't want to cut and run when I say I really need you to be my right hand from now on. More than ever, we need to have each other's backs. Are you cool with that?"

"Skipper, do you really have to ask? You know I have your back no matter what!"

"I know, but these aren't the operations we're used to. It's a lot to ask. We're about to explore things we never even thought possible until today."

"Clint, don't worry. I've always told you what I think; that's not going to change. I respect you as a professional and care about you as a friend. I'll continue to provide you with the same loyal commitment of my skills and my energy. So will the team. We're ready and willing to serve our country under your leadership. They chose the best man for the job."

Clint smiled, feeling more at ease. "Thanks, Master

Chief. I knew I could count on you. For now, I need you to take the team down to the lab and start familiarizing yourselves with the new tech that Doctor Rubin and Grace mentioned. Once you and I feel comfortable with the technical side and how everything works, we already have our first mission instructions."

"Well, don't just sit there. Spill the beans! What is it?"

"Hold on to your anchors, Master Chief. All in good time."

"You're the boss. I'll get the team and head down to the lab."

"Hold on, Paul. You can send Senior Chief Barnes down with the team to start learning the tech. You and I need to put our minds together and develop a prospective staff list to run this operation."

"Okay, you got it. I have a few favors I can call in back in Virginia, so I'll start building a command structure right away, starting with your assistant."

Paul stood and walked out of Clint's door to his own new office down the hall. He was ready to begin.

Clint sat back in his chair and took a long sip of coffee from his new coffeepot. *This is going to be some kind of ride.*

THE END . . . ?

Made in the USA
Columbia, SC
24 November 2021

49723322R00102